FRANK AND ELIZABETH

Patricia Thompson

AUGUST 4, 2014

AMAZON.COM

PATRICIA THOMPSON

ISBN-10: 0692259791
ISBN-13: 978-0692259795

DEDICATION

I would like to dedicate this book to my husband. For all the support and encouragement he gave me.

ACKNOWLEDGMENTS

I wish to thank my family for their support. I would also like to thank my Mother for her professionalism and editing skills she lent to this project.

CHAPTER 1

It was a dark and rainy Saturday afternoon. They were home enjoying a warm cozy fire. As they sat sipping wine, something seemed to be missing.

He looked at his wife with a puzzled expression. "Why haven't I heard the baby? I got home almost four hours ago."

A smile came over the face of his beautiful companion. "She is at your mother's house, remember?" She looked into his eyes and found a sense of loneliness. Returning the look with a similar gaze, "I know, I miss her too, but I do treasure our time alone together."

Frank and Elizabeth were enjoying their uninterrupted closeness. It was the first time in six months! Sabrina was away for her first evening with grandma, and they were having a hard time. Their whole lives were wrapped around their most precious gift. Sabrina was especially important to Frank because he lost his other children in a messy one-sided divorce.

Frank had been madly in love with his first wife, Sarah. They met at a party some friends were throwing. She was a beautiful college student, very particular in the company she kept. In a word, a snob. Sarah perceived him as a wild untamable man. As their friends introduced them, Sarah felt a strange curiosity come over her. She wanted to get to know him better. But Frank, was completely turned off by her. This made him all the more interesting. If she could just capture his attention, she felt she could tame him and learn from the strengths he seemed to possess. He was her new challenge, and *how* she loved a challenge.

Sarah was a law student. Her goal was to finish school and pass the Bar. Next week were her finals and soon after, she would take the Bar Exam. Frank gave her a new goal with a very handsome, almost unattainable prize. Right away her mind started working. First, she would need to get his attention. Sarah ran out and bought the tightest Wranglers she could squeeze her firm little butt in. Then, bought a sexy blouse and some red hot cowgirl boots.

So the game began. By talking to a few of their mutual friends, Sarah discovered he was working at the A and K Ranch, helping with riding lessons and pitching in where ever he could. She found the property starting on a long dirt road, just at the outskirts of town. As Sarah started down the road she thought to herself, "I'm off to meet my newest challenge!"

She found Frank in his usual state, working hard. He was of average height with a strong lean build (just the way she liked them). Sarah couldn't take her eyes off his shirtless glistening body. The sweat and the fact he had not even stopped to see who had approached him revealed to her what a hard-dedicated worker he was. It was apparent to her that Frank had been at it for hours with little or no break time. She stood staring for a moment. How could she not admire such a ruggedly handsome body?

"Excuse me, where do I go to sign up for riding lessons?" Sarah said, pretending to be lost.

"They're around the corner. Just keep go…" Frank was busy brushing a horse when he looked up to see who he was talking to. Right before his eyes was the most beautiful woman he had ever seen. Sarah's long shining auburn hair was swaying in the breeze. Her deep blue eyes sparkled, like diamonds in the sunlight. She had a perfect complexion, perfect body and a smile that would brighten the darkest night. This was an angel answering his prayers.

"Excuse me, ma'am," Frank said a little shaken. He forgot for a moment he was shirtless. Being the gentleman that he was, Frank took his shirt out of his back pocket, and proceeded to put it on. All of a sudden, a wave of impending darkness came over him and he shrugged it off.

Then realizing there was something familiar about her, Frank asked. "Have we met before?"

Sarah looked deep into his eyes with a dreamy expression. With a soft sultry voice, she said, "At a party last week."

Frank searched his memory. "Which party could she be talking about? I've been to four in the past week." Then he remembered, "She was the snob!" Frank wondered what would happen if they went out. Maybe they would find something in common. Even if they didn't, spending time with a beautiful woman couldn't be all bad. Looking back from his work Frank asked, "Would you like me to take you on tour by horseback, tomorrow? It's my day off."

"This is working out better than I thought," Sarah said to herself. She was ready to go anywhere with Frank. "Okay, I would like that." She said to Frank as a grin came over her face, but she wouldn't let him see. "What time would you like me here?"

"How 'bout around nine. I should be done with chores by then."

"I'll be here," was all Sarah could think to say. He somehow made her a little nervous, which made him all the more attractive.

Frank started wondering if it was such a good idea, but it was too late now.

At nine a.m. sharp, Sarah came sashaying in. Her beauty overcame any doubts Frank may have had about going through with their ride.

Frank had the horses saddled up and ready to go. He led Sarah on a ride to a beautiful meadow just beyond the forest that separated the ranch from the rest of the property. Her eyes lit up as they entered the tree line. A full cascade of morning sunshine flowed down through the leafy canopy. It illuminated the bright beautiful spring flowers that swept over the green rolling hills like a wave of rich vibrant color. Only to disappear into the rich greens of the forest that encircled the meadow. Frank told Sarah to sit quietly and look. Soon, she saw wild deer creep out of the forest. She couldn't believe her eyes. The deer were quiet and very observant. They soon took notice of Frank and Sarah watching and disappeared back into the woods. What an experience!

After watching the deer, Frank and Sarah rode to the banks of the Karanomi River. It was a fast moving, raging river. One of the natural boundaries of the A and K ranch. The water sparkled like a river of flowing diamonds. The Karanomi was so clear you could see the fish where the rocks tamed its mighty flow to a trickle.

Frank suggested they stop by the river's edge to have lunch. Then head back. It would take all week to explore the hundreds of acres, and hours to ride back to the barn. It was such a perfect spot. They could rest here and soak in the wonderful sights and sounds of nature.

Lunch consisted of bread, cheese, wine and grapes.

"This is wonderful!" Sarah thought to herself. She had never been treated this way. Sure, she had been taken to fancy restaurants and other nice places, but this was different. It took thought and planning. A beautiful spot, a romantic lunch and great conversation. Maybe there was more to him than she thought. This was already beyond her expectations.

"I'm happy you are enjoying your lunch. I wasn't sure what to pack." Frank was surprised to find she wasn't being the snob he had met at the party.

Frank and Sarah sat talking and sharing each other company for the rest of the afternoon. Frank noticed the sun starting to set. He looked at Sarah, "I know this great spot to watch the sunset. Would you like to see it?"

"I would love to."

Soon they were galloping up a hill. When Frank slowed his horse to a walk, Sarah followed. They sat on their horses overlooking the beautiful valley. The sunset was so magnificent from this view. It was a perfect ending to a perfect day.

Frank and Sarah wanted to see one another every day from that point on. The times apart became harder and harder to stand the more they saw each other. After three months of almost constant companionship they announced their engagement. Everyone was shocked! They seemed to be worlds apart from each other, but they were in love.

CHAPTER 2

Hard work and long hours were no stranger to Frank, and now he had something to work hard for. He invested his whole life into their marriage. Soon, after they were married, he changed jobs to increase his income.

Carpentry was a hidden talent, and with his business knowledge, Frank became the top foreman of Comstock Construction, a major fortune five hundred company. He was the superintendent, overseeing fifty crews, the largest in the company. His crews were sent to all the important jobs. They met or beat all their deadlines, but this meant ten to twelve hour days and a lot of Saturdays. Frank worked like this to give Sarah all the things she wanted to live comfortably.

Shortly after they were married, Sarah passed the bar exam and started bringing in an income. They decided to wait two years for children. That would give Sarah some time to find a firm and give her a full year in her law practice. She would be able to establish herself and they would have a good nest egg saved.

Frank and Sarah started out in a small studio apartment. It worked out for them, since they both were starting with little, and it was close to work. They ate out only once a month; just for a break. If they had wanted to they could have easily eaten out twice a week and had a nice apartment. This way they could have their house much sooner.

Finally, after a year and a half went by they looked into their finances and found they could afford a house. While they were figuring out what they could afford, Sarah told Frank she had a surprise for him. When she left the room Frank got out a surprise for Sarah. To their amazement they had the same surprise. Frank and Sarah had been putting money away on the side. They put all the money together and found they could afford to own the ranch they had always wanted.

It was beautiful. Frank and Sarah decided to name it The Pine-Mountain-River Ranch. From the deck of the new house you could see land for miles. At the edge of the vast view there were mountains. Mountains that seemed to shoot out of the ground and stand there so tall, as to show off how magnificent they were. There were rolling hills of high mountain pines with the fragrance of Christmas all year long. These handsome pines surrounded meadows with the greenest, sweetest smelling spring grass and the biggest brightest flowers. It was a dream come true. Frank and Sarah were so happy. One hundred and fifty acres is a lot to take care of, but all the hard work would be worth it.

Sarah would have to commute part time and could work from home the rest of the time. Frank relocated to a company nearer the ranch. This allowed him to devote a lot of time to the property. Because soon, not only would the meadows and pastures be filled with steer and Mustangs, but with the hopes and dreams of a brighter future for their children.

Frank and Sarah worked very hard to make their ranch a success. After three long years Frank quit his job to manage their large herd of steer and large herd of wild horses. They had everything they needed to complete their happy lives except children. Frank and Sarah were becoming worried. What would happen if they couldn't have children? Sarah started checking into some fertility clinics. But before she could make an appointment, she found out she was pregnant. Soon after, they were blessed with a baby boy. He was named John Martin. It had been four long years and three months after they were married. Frank and Sarah hoped they wouldn't have to wait so long for their next one. Joyfully, two years later, they were blessed again! This time with a wonderful baby girl. She was named Phyllis Kindra.

Sarah fell in love, instantly, each time she saw one of the babies, for the first time. She was a very loving and caring mother. They took first place to everything, including Frank. He was happy with the way Sarah felt. The children, he thought, should take first place.

It would have been close to impossible to find another father so devoted to his children. Frank loved the outdoors. He spent many hours teaching his children the ways of nature. The ranch allowed many opportunities for him to share the wonders of a natural world to them. Frank would take the children, John and Phyllis, to find a camping spot on Friday. Then Sarah would meet them that night. The family would hike and fish all weekend. They had many favorite outdoor activities, but their favorite of all was waterskiing.

Each year Frank would work extra hard to reach a financial goal. One year it was a trip. Another year it was paying off some big bills. For their sixth year of marriage, Frank bought the family a ski boat. The family spent many hours on the water. With the boat, Frank was able to take the time to teach Sarah to ski. She was a natural.

Phyllis watched her mother learning. This sparked her interest, and she decided to try it out. After that Frank couldn't teach her fast enough. Every day she wanted to be on the water. Phyllis became very good in a short time. By the time she was eight, Frank could see definite possibilities forming.

Phyllis loved spending time with her father. Alone with him she was herself, it was her favorite time. When the weather or time didn't allow skiing, they would go to the movies, shop at downtown stores or go to the batting cages. Much of their time was spent outdoors fishing, canoeing and waterskiing. Frank and Phyllis' time together was an opportunity to learn many things from each other. Most of all, it was their time.

John was a very shy boy. Learning to climb and repel from his father, and helping him teach others, was the only way to get John to come out his shell. He was ten at this time and was becoming very experienced. John and his father made quite an impressive team. Frank would explain how to repel and how to be safe. Then John would demonstrate that anyone of any age could do it. The children would feel better seeing a young person repelling with such ease. Frank got a lot of enjoyment out of climbing and repelling. He was happy to share it with John. This gave them an opportunity to have some special father/son time.

Frank was very thankful for the family he was given. Everything he did was wrapped around them. Even when he was gone from them, all Frank could think of was: 'How are they doing? What are they doing?' Or 'I wish I could share what I am doing/seeing with them.' Frank was not whole without them. All of the time he spent with his family was cherished.

One Saturday, the last normal Saturday of his life, Frank was hit with a big shock. Things would never be the same again. This Saturday started out just like all the others. The kids came in to wake them up. Frank and Sarah took their showers and got dressed. Then sent the kids to take showers and get ready for the day, as they went downstairs. Soon Phyllis and John came down for breakfast. While they were all sitting around the table finishing up; Sarah announced she was taking the children to see her dad and mom. The children were very excited, they loved grandpa and grandma!

This was not like Sarah to make plans for the day and not discuss them with Frank, at least let him know what was going on. He took her aside and asked why she was taking the children to their grandparents. Sarah told him they needed some time together, alone, to talk. It was true things had not been going well between them lately. So off she went with the children. Sarah returned about an hour later. Trying to gather her thoughts and regain her composer, she sat in the car for quite some time.

Frank knew something was wrong and ran out to the car. "Are you okay? What happened? What's wrong?"

Sarah tried to hide that she was crying, but she couldn't. It was clear to her that he thought she was physically injured. "I'm not hurt, but something is wrong. It's between us." She paused not knowing what to say.

"What is it? What have I done?" Frank was perplexed. He assumed it was his fault, whatever it was. Because, as of lately, she was always finding ways to be upset with him. He knew they were going through a rough patch, but she was truly crying. Something wasn't right. The next thing Sarah said came out of left field.

"I…it…it's over." The words barely made it out, but she had to tell him. "I don't know what else to do. I love you, but I can't handle living with you anymore."

Sarah still loved him. It gave Frank hope. Even if it was just a little hope. He was in shock and didn't know what to say. He needed her! He needed his family! "You can't do this. What have I done? Am I such a bad husband? Why am I so hard to live with?" Frank was getting angry. "Have I ever hurt you? Do I make your life miserable? Haven't I done everything for you and our family? What about our children?" Frank was so angry he was yelling and firing off questions as fast as they came to him.

"Sto-o-op!" Sarah screamed! "I can't do this anymore! Everything is an argument with you, and I'm always the bad guy. I can't see who I want to see. I can't talk to whomever I want to talk to. I can't do anything without your permission. You should put up with, my friends. Just like I put up with, yours. The good ones and the bad ones. Nothing I do is good enough for you! You, are not always right. And I can't take it anymore! You have taught me to be strong, and stand up for myself. Now is the time for me to do just that. I want you to leave." Sarah started to cry. "I need you out of my life. I don't know what else to say. I just…" She couldn't it hold back anymore, the sobs just came tumbling.

Frank stood staring with a blank expression. He was stunned. Things had not been quite right lately, but he had no idea Sarah was so unhappy. "Can we try? We need to work this out." Now Frank's voice was soft and she could hear his sincerity. "I love you with all my heart and soul, but more important than us, the children need us to be a family."

Sarah thought to herself for a moment. "If I don't do something Frank will talk me into staying together. We can't stay together. Things would get better, for a while. But then, as always, he will go back to being impossible." Sarah, having no intention of trying to work it out, said, "I still love you; that will never change. I can't go on like this, but maybe we could try a little longer. I just need some space. Why don't you move out for a while?" Frank's eyes looked so sad. "Or maybe you could go fishing for a week. Just to give us time. Time to think about our relationship. The children could stay with me. I am sure they could also spend some of the time with my dad and mom."

"Okay, I agree it would be better if we had time to think. A week seems like a long time away, but if you need that much time, okay. We will talk as soon as I get back. You can count on that." Frank was hesitant, but agreed feeling it was the only chance they had to work it out. They had rough patches before, and he hoped this was just another one. If it was more than that, Frank, would fight with everything to keep their family together.

The following day Frank said good-bye to Sarah and his children. Then he set out for a week of fishing with his best friend Bruce.

Bruce took a week off work, and told his wife he'd see her when he got back. He didn't tell her why; just that he needed to go. Most wives would have been angry. She knew he wouldn't take off without giving her details unless it was the way it needed to be done. So when Bruce said good-bye, his wife he just said, 'I love you' and 'I'll see you when you get back.'

This fishing trip was very different from any other in the past. Usually, the mood is very light and happy. It was a time to get away from all the pressures of everyday life. Their time away allowed them the opportunity to do things that wouldn't be appropriate at home, such as: Drinking beer until you can't stand up, telling dirty nasty jokes, being too loud and the, 'you can't do that around the children', types of things. It gave them their own space without the responsibilities of home. But this time was different, this time it was very quiet in the jeep, Frank was lonely for his family. It wasn't his choice to go on a fishing trip this time.

When Frank and Bruce arrived at the spot they unloaded the jeep and set out to fish. This time there was more talking than serious fishing. The trip continued pretty much the same as the week went on. Frank would sit quietly thinking, or he would ask Bruce a bunch of 'what do you think?' questions.

By the time the week ended, Frank, had figured out a few things. He realized how his time was spent. Up at 5am to care for the animals. Then he would come in to make breakfast about 7am. Feed the kids and get them off to school. About that time Sarah would come down in a rush, with just enough time to say good-bye to Frank, and dash off to work. Thinking about this made him shake his head in disgust. If she wasn't out so late the night before, Sarah would be up spending time with the kids before school and work, the way it used to be.

After a hard day's work, Frank would greet the children as they got home. He would get dinner ready while they were in their rooms doing homework. At 6pm dinner would be ready and on the table. Sarah was almost never there. Most days she was out until very late in the evening. She was either out with 'clients' or blowing off steam with friends from work. Their family time was disappearing as Sarah spent more and more time away from home. Even their family outings were few and far between. Her friends were single or unhappily married and seemed to be a bad influence on her. That was why he didn't want her to see or hang out with certain people. His concern over Sarah's absentness and the deteriorating family time was the reason most fights started. The children were even noticing. Frank was very frustrated. He just wanted his family to be together, the way it used to be.

Frank came to a decision, no matter what it took he would take whatever chance Sarah gave him. He missed her. Most of all, Frank needed John and Phyllis. He never wanted anything to come between him and his family, ever.

When Frank returned from his fishing trip he a lot to tell Sarah. He had a new understanding of their situation. But when he got there, the house was empty. Frank put his things away. Then he headed into the kitchen to make a snack, hoping his family would return soon. On the refrigerator was a note. It read:

Frank,

> **Please leave tomorrow by 4pm. The children and I will be back then.**
> **It is definitely over. My lawyer will be contacting you over at your sister's. DON'T try and contact me; I have a restraining order filed against you.**

> **Sarah**

Frank was pissed! "She not only left with the children, but she got a restraining order too?! What does she think I'm going to do?" Frank decided, if she went to all that trouble to keep him away, he would let her alone. He was still clinging to the hope she might change her mind.

* * * * * * * * * * * * * *

Some years later, looking back from a different perspective, Frank was able to figure it out. All of Sarah's reasons for leaving, she made up, to cover what Frank had figured out much later. He had known something deceptive was going on, but didn't know what she was hiding. Later, he found out about the affairs. She was always looking for the next best thing. In the end she never found anyone better than Frank.

The restraining order puzzled him for a long time. It was very damaging to Frank's reputation, not that what people thought of him ever really mattered, but to do that took someone very cruel. Frank never saw her as a cruel person. One of Sarah's friends told him, long after her murder, it was just another way to keep him from his kids. Sarah made up a story that she was afraid of Frank. She was very convincing. The court issued it, but when they went before the judge, he saw through her and dropped it, due to lack of proof. Everything Sarah did was to have power and control over Frank's life.

* * * * * * * * * * * * *

He called his friend Bruce and asked if he could stay with him for a while. Frank packed a few things and left a note. It told the children he loved them and Sarah where she could reach him. Time to leave. Frank took a long look around. He hoped to be back home with his family very soon.

Unfortunately, after all the talking, mediation and fighting and more mediation there was more of the same. Then came the real lawyers and general bullshit. After that, the paperwork, and more bullshit. It was all too much for Frank. Worst of all, the children were suffering. Assuming that Sarah had all their best interests at heart, Frank left the final legalities up to her.

It was a bad idea. Sarah showed her true colors. She was very self-absorbed, and became vindictive. She left him without anything of value except for some very personal possessions that he had before they were married. Sarah, on the other hand, had the children and power over when and where they could see their father. She also had all the possessions they took ten years to build up together. Most of them, just like the ranch, she sold!

Frank could not decide if he was more sad or angry. He didn't care about the *things* he lost, but anguished everyday over the loss of his children. Some days he would sit and stare into space remembering the happy life he so recently lost.

Seeing the children was close to impossible. Sarah made sure of that. Between the restraining order and her lack of communication, Frank only saw them a few times the first year they were divorced. Every time he tried to contact the children, Sarah would make sure Frank couldn't. Eventually, she realized what she thought she wanted, wasn't.

Sarah reached a point where she was really missing Frank, and decided the divorce was a big mistake. By that time, Frank had decided he would never trust her again. Sarah called Frank one day and asked him back. He said no, after all she put him through. He couldn't. That was the end of it all.

Sarah moved and never let Frank know her whereabouts. Anyone that might have known, wasn't telling. Sarah was a very good liar and made Frank out to be an awful ex-husband. She told everyone he was jealous and wouldn't let her alone. With so much against him, and not wanting to confuse his children and disrupt their lives any further, Frank gave into Sarah and quit trying. He figured, when they were ready, the children would come to him. After all the love and devotion he gave them, as young children, they should surely remember his love for them.

This was very hard for Frank, but he let John and Phyllis go. He had hoped they wouldn't have the constant conflict in their lives that Frank had as a child. There was so much conflict around him while he was growing up. Frank made a vow never to expose his family to the rigors and pain of the life he knew as a youngster.

CHAPTER 3

Frank's father did many hard years in the war. They left him an angry bitter man. The government trained him to defend himself and his country. When he came home life was so different. With all their training, the military forgot to teach them how to cope with all the stress that came with being a soldier. He saw death. The death of fellow soldiers, his friends, strangers and even the enemy. It was supposed to be, 'just a part of the war', but he knew many of the deaths were senseless. There was so much anger, pain and death, but through all the chaos he found some way to reason it all. Until he got state side.

The military was the only place he ever felt at home. Even though he loved the military. They trained him and taught him discipline. Frank's father didn't always agree with their policies. Often, his father disagreed with his superiors. Yet, he had no choice, but to follow orders. Judgment was not allowed by anyone. His duty, his job, was all that matter to the military.

All his life growing up Frank's father was treated as a failure. Being the exceptional soldier that he was, everything he did, was a job well done. Each pat on the back was conformation that he wasn't a failure. That he fit in. That he belonged.

Frank's father couldn't help feeling a rush every time he killed the enemy. Knowing that he had escaped his own death, and death was around every corner. The adrenalin rush from the 'hunt or be hunted' kills made him feel a live. It was mission accomplished. At the end of the day he felt good and exhausted. It was a simple and exciting way to live.

Frank's father did his job knowing he would be left in some backwoods country, alone, if he didn't do his job. Most of his missions were covert and not officially recognized by the government. There wasn't a rescue party coming if they got into trouble. He took lives in order to live another day. In the heat of it all coping was easy. Just think of the next mission. It was a different story when he returned to civilian life. Coping was very difficult. Frank's father used the only coping mechanism the military ever taught him, alcohol. At home he started drinking to unwind, just like after a mission or when he had down time. But when the restless nights started and the nightmares, it became his best friend.

Frank's mother was good woman. She loved Frank's father. They met before he joined the service and dated off and on throughout his training and tours. When he came home the last time they married. When Frank was born his parents were overjoyed. Soon after the birth she was pregnant again, this time they had a baby girl. Frank's mother was so happy, she always wanted a large family. A year went by and again she was pregnant, but this time she lost the baby. Complications made it impossible for them to have another one. Frank's parents were very sad and never got over the loss. Frank's mother learned to cope with it, but his father just slipped into a deep depression.

While Frank was growing up his mother was a constant bright light in his life. She was always there for him. His father, however, tried very hard to be a good and loving parent, but with all the scars, depression and drinking, it was too hard. Frank's father retreated into himself. It was a hard childhood for anyone.

Frank tried, but he couldn't relate to his father. Things were too much for him. So, at sixteen, he left home. He tried to find a happier life, and take some of the financial burden off his family. Frank was bound and determined his sister would have the money to go to college if she wanted.

It didn't take long for him to find a job. Frank found he could go from city to city and work odd jobs. He made good money and had a lot of freedom. The only contact with his family were monthly calls to his mother and a check here and there to help her with the bills.

Frank moved around a lot because he would get bored or find himself in trouble, usually for defending what he believed in. He learned one very important lesson from his father: "Always stand up for what you believe in. Don't let people push you around."

One of the longest jobs he had was for the railroad. Frank loved the freedom it gave him. He would travel along the country side laying track. This gave him a good pay check, and an opportunity to travel beyond the small cities he had been traveling to. After three long years with the railroad, Frank was laid off. There wasn't enough work for the workforce. After sending money home, he was left with a small savings account and no job. The railroad offered to pay his way home, but he just pocketed the travel money and stayed in Carson City, Nevada.

Frank put most of the money in the bank, and went to find a new job, a new adventure. He went from farm to farm asking for work. It didn't matter if the job was big or small, clean or dirty, he just wanted to work. In the first week he plowed a field, started a room addition and dug an irrigation ditch. Frank decided he liked the work. He just had to find something permanent. That's when he saw an advertisement for a ranch hand in the local paper. The add read:

THE A AND K RANCH
HIRING ALL-AROUND COWBOYS.
ROOM AND BOARD. WEEKLY PAY.
EXPECT LONG HOURS AND HARD WORK.
MEET AT THE MAIN CORRAL. SUNUP.

This looked like a good deal to Frank. He found a place to camp for the night and got ready for the next day.

It was dark when he woke and packed his gear. Frank walked five miles to the A and K Ranch. He reached the corral just after dawn. No one seemed to be around. Thinking it was too late, Frank started to leave.

"Just a minute!" Frank heard a voice calling after him. As he stopped and turned around a man approached Frank. "Are you here about the job?"

"Yes I am."

The man sized up Frank. "You are late, but we need one more man. Can you ride?"

"Some."

"Are you afraid of hard work?"

"No, sir."

"Can you learn?"

"I catch on pretty fast."

"Well then, I think you might work out just fine. I'm Mr. Walters, the owner of this ranch."

"Glad to meet you. I'm Frank. Thanks for the chance."

After they shook hands and went over the details, Mr. Walters took Frank on a short tour of the ranch. They ended at the stables. Frank set to work as soon as his duties were explained.

Frank liked the long hours and hard work. It felt good to be exhausted at the end of the day. He loved the outdoors and the freedom of working without someone constantly looking over his shoulder. It was a wonderful job.

CHAPTER 4

Frank worked at the A and K Ranch for about six months before he met Sarah. He had no idea how his life would change. Frank never expected to get married, let alone, have children or ever get divorced. After working hard and building his own ranch, he found himself alone, without a family. Right back where he started, when he left his boyhood home. But this time he was sad and empty. He had made his family his whole life; now his life was gone.

Frank decided he had to start over. Montana would be his new home. Frank had never been there before, but he figured he could go off in the wilderness, if he had a mind to. That was just the freedom from the world and everyday life he needed from time to time.

Frank hopped on a train and made his way to Montana. The state was more beautiful than he had ever imagined. He found a hotel, got a newspaper and settled in. He looked, but couldn't find work in town. After a week of papers and walking the streets of town, Frank decided to widen his search. He went from town to town. Looking everywhere. Three weeks went by. Frank was about to give up and go back to his mother's. When he stumbled into a logging town.

"This is perfect!" Frank was very hopeful. He asked around and found the logging foreman's office. Just missing the foreman, Frank took his gear and found a place to camp nearby.

The next day, Frank woke at dawn, happy to find people all ready to start work. He packed his gear and headed for the foreman's office. Frank was told the hours would be long and hard. It was music to Frank's ears. The foreman put him to work as a tree bucker.

This was a new experience, so he started at the bottom. Frank was pared with an experienced tree bucker. The man showed him how to buck a tree. The logger takes a chain saw, walks down a fallen tree and knocks off the branches. It is one of the preparations needed so that the loader can put the logs on the log truck. It was dangerous because if the log rolled, the man on it might fall off and get crushed.

Frank enjoyed living in the logging camp. Every day was full of hard work and the beauty of the woods. At night he was exhausted. He hadn't slept this well in months. It felt good to be on his own, making his own way, but Frank really missed his children.

Many times at night he would lay awake thinking back to the wonderful times he had with his children. When his thoughts began Frank was happy, but soon his mood would change to sadness and anger. He couldn't understand how Sarah could have taken away his children. He was never mean to them. In fact, Frank doted on them.

Frank made up his mind. He would work very hard until he could take Sarah back to court. HE WOULD NOT LIVE THE REST OF HIS LIFE WITHOUT HIS CHILDREN!!

Frank worked very hard. Improving all the time. Soon he was promoted to sectioning the trees. After the tree was cut down and bucked, Frank would walk along the log and cut it into sections. Then the logs where loaded onto the log truck. Next he was taught how to cut a tree down and make it fall just exactly where he wanted it to. Soon as he had mastered his new skills, Frank's boss informed him there was a position opening up for a foreman. Frank put in for it and got it. With this promotion came a pay raise. All the extra money he made was saved, except for a small amount that Frank continued to send home to his mother.

After five years of working hard and saving every dime, Frank finally had the money he would need to hire a lawyer. Before he could look into legal counsel, he had a few preparations to make. First he would go into town and find a decent place to live. Frank decided to go on Saturday morning. With some concrete decisions made, Frank felt better and was able to get some rest.

Saturday came way too slow, but Frank worked all the extra hours he could. He was up, showered and dressed in his best duds by 4am. Now what? He was too early to go talk to anyone. So he decided to go to the town's only all-night diner. To grab breakfast and the morning paper, and get a jumpstart on the house hunting.

By eight o'clock, Frank had driven by six houses. He had a pretty good idea of what he could afford and what he wanted. Now it was time to see a real estate broker. It wasn't hard to choose. There was only one office open in town, the rest didn't open until nine or ten. Being the first one open impressed Frank, immensely.

He walked into a brightly lit office. The smell of hot fresh coffee surrounded him with a blanket of warmth and welcome. Frank moseyed on over to the desk where a bright cheery smile greeted him. She was beautiful, but Frank tried not to notice. The last thing on his list was another relationship.

"Hello. Welcome to Mountain Top Realty. My name is Elizabeth Miller, how may I be of service to you?"

Frank smiled and shook her extended hand. "Howdy, I'm Frank. I am lookin' to buy a house." He proceeded to explain the size and styles he was interested in. They talked for a while. Then went to look at some prospects.

Frank and Miss Miller went house to house all day long. When they were finished Frank made an appointment with Miss Miller to see more houses the next weekend. There were a couple he wanted to see again. One in particular, was a modest three bedroom ranch style on a three acre lot. There would be enough room for him and his children.

Frank worked hard all that week. Time passed quickly. Soon it was the weekend. As he drove into town he found himself looking forward to seeing Miss Miller almost as much as finding a suitable house. Frank and Miss Miller spent all day looking. Somewhere around five p.m. Frank asked if he could take Miss Miller out for something to eat. She agreed.

They went to a cozy little seafood and steak house. The meal was wonderful and so was the company. By the time the evening was over, Frank had decided on the house he wanted and the woman he wanted.

It was something he hadn't expected. Even after five years, Frank had thought he would never want another relationship. The feelings he felt were scary, but he was happy to have them back. He didn't feel quite so alone anymore.

The next four months Frank spent the weeks working and the weekends in town. During this time, Frank decided to wait on the house. Sarah had moved, again. But this time it was taking longer to find her and the children. He had kept tabs on them in the past, but lost track long enough for them to slip away. Frank was confident that he would pick up their trail again, but until then the house would wait.

All his extra time was spent with Miss Miller. As time passed, they became closer and closer. Miss Miller came to be known as Elizabeth to Frank.

It was hard to trust a woman. No matter how honest she was. After Sarah, every woman seemed devious. Elizabeth was a very patient woman. Something Sarah never was. Frank found himself trusting her and falling in love. Scared as he was, Frank found himself telling her very personal things. Things he had never told anyone else, not even Sarah. It was a monumental step for Frank.

One evening as they were walking in the moonlight, Frank told Elizabeth of his children, John and Phyllis, and his ex-wife. He had concealed it from her. The loss of his children was just too hard to talk about. But Frank, being at ease with Elizabeth, found comfort in telling her about his children, the divorce and how things had gone wrong in their marriage.

Elizabeth was very understanding, but found herself having some disconcerting feelings. There were many unanswered questions and feelings that were becoming too strong to ignore. Finally, love, the feelings of confusion and Frank's inability to trust anyone, made Elizabeth decide to take a break from the relationship for a short while.

When Elizabeth told Frank of her feelings he was unhappy. "At least," Frank said to himself, "I know now that she isn't afraid to be honest with me."

Frank had been feeling a little apprehensive also. He agreed a little time a part was good. It would be hard, but good.

The next week was lonely. He buried himself deep into his work. Along with all the regular work, Frank picked up extra busy work, but time still felt like it was passing as slow as a snail crossing the road. Elizabeth had an equally difficult task trying to get time to pass. A week went by, they found themselves so miserable that time apart was not working.

Elizabeth came to Frank one day and told him they needed to have a serious talk about their feelings. They talked for many hours about everything they liked and didn't like about each other, their pasts and other things on their minds. When they finished many things were worked out. The rest would be worked out later. They promised: To be patient with each other. To discuss everything that was bothering them. And to be quiet and understanding when the other one had something to talk about.

They were so much in love. Their talk was great for clearing the air, and it matured their relationship. Frank and Elizabeth spent the rest of the afternoon at the movie theater watching the latest comedy and enjoying each other's company. It was nice to spend a couple of hours together without the pressure of talking (their discussion was very exhausting).

After the movie, they decided to part and catch up to with each other the next day. Frank was relieved to have time alone to mull over their talk. Elizabeth felt very lonely the rest of the evening. She had been so afraid that they were at the end of their relationship. When she found they were at a new beginning. All she wanted, was to spend the rest of the evening cuddled in Frank's arms.

CHAPTER 5

The next morning Frank was excited, but wouldn't tell Elizabeth why. He took her out for breakfast. Then told her he had business to tend to. She was very disappointed not to spend the day with Frank, but it was for work. It had to get done, and by him. "At least," he told her, "I'm getting' a bonus."

Understanding, Elizabeth agreed to meet Frank, later that evening for dinner. Promising to take her to the fanciest restaurant in town; he said he'd pick her up at five o'clock and they would have the rest of the evening together.

So the two of them parted company. Frank went straight home. Elizabeth decided to shop for a new dress. She hadn't bought one in almost two years. The old ones in the closet seemed to do fine most of the time, but his was a special occasion with a very special man. It took her all afternoon to find the perfect dress, with the perfect accessories. Elizabeth arrived home just in time to take a shower. Then do her hair and makeup. She wanted to look perfect.

Frank showed up at five o'clock on the dot, and was dressed very handsomely in a western style tux with new boots and new Stetson. Elizabeth opened the door wearing a red velvet dress. It fit very well and reached almost to the floor. The dress was finished with red satin trim, and a slit half way up her thigh.

Frank's chin almost hit the floor. "I've never seen ya look purdier." He said in his sexy southern drawl.

"Why, thank you, sir." Elizabeth replied with a winkle in her eye, and her own attempt at a southern drawl. She was very happy, and got just the response she was looking for.

"Dinner's awaitin'." Frank was so excited and nervous about his plans for after dinner. He just wanted to get through it and on with his plans.

Dinner was lovely: Wonderful food, romantic candle light and someone playing piano quietly in the corner. Frank could tell Elizabeth was pleased. He hoped the evening would turn out as perfect as that very moment.

After dinner, they went outside and took a stroll through the woods. He stopped her as they reached a bench facing a beautiful moon lit pond. Taking her hands, Frank looked deeply into her eyes. "Elizabeth, I have a very serious offer for you. I want you to give it a lot of thought." He took a deep breath. "My mother is ill."

The words came out of left field. "What a strange thing to say." Thought Elizabeth. She was sure he was about to propose. Then panic struck her. Was Frank going to leave her? How long? Was he ever coming back? As many disturbing thoughts raced through her head, Frank broke in.

"My sister called and needs my help. I spoke with Ma. I'll go help her and stay until she is well enough to take care of things herself. She offered to loan me money for land to start a ranch. I can be near her and realize my dream of owning a ranch again. And I want you to come with me." Frank paused, allowing it all to sink in. He removed his hat and got down on one knee. "Miss Elizabeth Miller, would you be so kind, as to accompany me through the rest of my days?"

Elizabeth looked at Frank. She looked for a long while. Finally, she said, "I love you. Of 'course I'll marry you. And don't you worry about your mother, she's as good as well."

Frank was overjoyed! He was so worried she wouldn't want to leave her job to help care for an ailing mother-in-law. One she had never met. Soon as Elizabeth had said yes, Frank, felt reassured. She was just the woman he had been looking for. He loved Elizabeth, but after Sarah, Frank knew there needed to be more to the relationship than just a strong love. Elizabeth showed Frank a devotion to him and his family that no one had ever come close to before. It cinched it for him.

She put in her two weeks' notice and her house up for sale. Elizabeth was put in charge of moving arrangements. It was a lot of work. She arranged a moving company to pick up and deliver all their things to a storage near Frank's mother's house. Now she had the daunting task of packing and organizing. Elizabeth had to decide what went to storage and what went with her and Frank.

Elizabeth knew that she and Frank would have the basement. That would give them a lot of room and privacy, and allowed them to be close to his mother. There were many things that had to be put away, but what to keep, what to sell, what to throw out? These were hard decisions, but in the end she got through it all.

Most of her furniture had to go and kitchen gadgets plus many other things. So after the packing, sorting, and moving things into storage, Elizabeth had a three day estate sale. She sold many things she had been collecting over the years, some from her childhood. When the sale was done; Elizabeth made over $1,000.00. Paid some bills and put $500.00 into an account she didn't tell Frank about. Elizabeth was big on saving money and wanted to put some back in case they needed a little help.

Frank had told his boss he had to leave and why. It was close to the end of the season so he didn't need to give much notice. His boss was sorry to see him go.

"If you're lookin' for work next season, you'll have a job here," Frank's boss said.

Frank left early to see his mother and get things set up. He wanted things as ready as possible before Elizabeth arrived. This would be a big adjustment for her and he wanted to make it as easy as possible.

A week before moving day Elizabeth called Frank. In an excited voice she said, "Frank, I need to ask you something," as soon as she heard his voice on the other end. "I know you asked me to marry you… and… I want to. But we haven't planned a day, or a time. I want to start out our life together right. I don't want to live under your mother's roof unwed."

"It will be okay. One of us can live in the apartment and the other one can stay in a room upstairs until we are married." Elizabeth really hadn't thought that far. She felt very foolish.

"Thank you. Do you think we could get married in a little ceremony at your mother's house? Your sister could stand up for me and your mother would be there as a witness. It would be a very special day. "

"That would be wonderful, but are you sure you don't want time to plan a big wedding with both families and all our friends."

Elizabeth knew Frank well enough to know that he really would rather have a very small wedding. He was just trying to make her happy. "I would really like to be married sooner than later. If we want, later, we can have a reception party with all our family and friends." Frank was much happier to hear Elizabeth say that. It took a lot of pressure off the whole situation.

Frank called his sister. After explaining to her, she offered to make all the arrangements for a wedding at their mother's house the following week. "Are you sure it gives you two enough time?" Frank's sister knew how important it was to them, to start their new life together, right.

"It will give us plenty of time. The simpler and sooner the better." Frank stated with conviction. "Can you come here tomorrow? I'll be able to help you at that time."

The next day Frank started setting up the basement. He had been cleaning it out and was finally done. He was relieved to get a lot accomplished during the week, but missed seeing Elizabeth every day. She was missing him too.

Soon it was Saturday. Frank was there to help and they got to see each other. It was time to load the moving truck. Elizabeth was very excited to be starting her new adventure. First, she and Frank loaded the things that would go with them. Next came the things for storage; things to be saved for their future. It was hard to get things done as quickly as they wanted to because they found themselves lost in conversation, or at times, just in each other's glance.

Today was an exciting, but nerve racking day. Elizabeth had never met Frank's mother or sister. She was secure knowing Frank loved her and would do his best to make their lives better. To make their dreams come true. So Elizabeth was content to wait until the time their true future could be realized. She would spend as many months or years needed to help his mother. But even though she made her mind up, Elizabeth was still a bit nervous.

After the storage was full they were on their way. As they drove along they talked about their new situation. Frank was trying to explain things. He was very nervous that Elizabeth was taking on more than she expected or she might not get along with his mother and sister. Her happiness was very important to him.

Elizabeth could see Frank was nervous and his mind kept drifting. "Can we stop at the next town? I would like a cup of coffee and a short break."

"Okay, but we only have a couple more hours to go." Frank could see she wanted to stop. At the next town he pulled off the highway and into the nearest gas station.

"Where to next?" Frank asked expecting her to suggest a coffee house.

"Just follow my directions, please?" Elizabeth wasn't sure if Frank would do it. She didn't want to have to explain it to him, so shot him an 'I really want to, but please don't ask, look'. Whatever Frank saw in her eyes worked. Because he didn't ask, just followed her directions. Until, she said, "Turn in here."

"What are we doing here?"

"I want to do a little shopping before we get to your mom's." Frank followed Elizabeth in. He wasn't sure if he was happy with the side trip or not, but they had time and she was happy.

It was a western style clothing store. Every kind of western wear you could think of, they had it.

"Let's look over here." Elizabeth grabbed Frank's arm and guided in the direction of dressy men's western wear. "I've been saving money for a while for this. I want us to get nice outfits for Wednesday."

"Well of course we can, I saved some money to get you a nice dress too. I just didn't know when we would get time to shop." Frank was very happy.

After looking through the men's clothing for a while, Elizabeth decided to go check out the dresses. Frank kept looking for the perfect shirt. About an hour passed, by this time Frank had his outfit at the register and had been looking at other things just wasting time waiting, when an attendant came to get him and asked him to follow her.

Frank smiled when he saw Elizabeth. She must have tried on every dress there. The one she had on was beautiful. "It's perfect."

"I really like this one, and I found shoes to go with it." She said with a big smile on her face.

Next Elizabeth showed Frank some beautiful silver combs she found for his mother. She also found a necklace and earrings for his sister. On the way to the register, Elizabeth talked Frank into a new straw hat. He hadn't bought a new straw in almost fifteen years; his had definitely been around. It was hard to get him to buy new things, but Frank did like to have quality. Elizabeth was very happy and ready to go to her new home and start her new life!

CHAPTER 6

They pulled up the long driveway, and there in a clearing, was the most beautiful house and yard. It was an old two story farm house with gingerbread trim, dormer windows and rap around deck on both levels. As Elizabeth emerged from the truck, she was greeted with the aroma of roses and lavender from the flower gardens on both sides of the walkway.

Frank and Elizabeth came to the front door of the magnificent house and rang the bell. Soon as the door opened, any fears that Elizabeth may have had, melted away. There standing in front of them was the sweetest looking elderly lady. Even with her walker you could tell she was not a weak push over. Her smile let Elizabeth know that this lady would earn the name, mom, before the day was out.

"Well, hello you two. This must be Elizabeth. Frank told me quite a bit about you."

"He told me a lot about you too. All good things." Elizabeth said with a smile.

"Come in. Come in. Frank your sister went into town to get some things for dinner. She thought we should spoil you tonight." Frank's mother said to them. Then she turned to Elizabeth. "Call me mom if you like, or Madeline if you're more comfortable."

"I'll call you mom, if you call me Lizzy. Only people close to my heart call me Lizzy." Elizabeth was very happy she was so well received by Frank's mom.

Frank showed Elizabeth his room from childhood. "This is where I will stay until we are married a week from Wednesday. You take the master suite. Mom will be in the room down stairs. That way she won't have to use the stairs, and we have the upstairs."

"Will you unload my suit cases? I want to get a few things unpacked before I help your sister with dinner." Frank smiled and started to leave to get the cases. But Lizzy stopped him, just long enough, to give him a smooch. "Thank you."

Elizabeth freshened up and headed down stairs to find Madeline. "How are you feeling this afternoon?"

"Oh, hello dear. I'm feeling well. Just a little tired. Thank you for asking. I thought you'd be resting after such a busy day."

"No, Frank's unloading a couple of my suit cases so I can start getting settled in. I just wanted to say thank you for your warm welcome and the use of the upstairs. I also wanted to know if there were any special things I need to know about the house or your routine or anything else that might be important. I'm sure most things Frank and Rose can tell me, but this is your house and you're the one we came to help. So you tell me any of the things that are important to you."

"Why aren't you sweet? There are a few things." Madeline told Elizabeth her daily routine, her pet peeves and some of the quirks of the old house. Then Elizabeth asked how soon Rose would be returning and to have Frank come and get her so she might help with dinner.

The rest of the evening went along very well. Frank, Elizabeth, Rose and Madeline all enjoyed each other's company. That evening after Rose left for home and Madeline was settled in for the night, Frank and Elizabeth took a stroll in the moonlight. It was very romantic. Then Frank walked Elizabeth to her bedroom door and said good night. It felt a bit strange but sweet in a quirky sort of way.

The next week went by fast. There was a new routine to learn, for Elizabeth. Frank started work at a local ranch. Soon it was the day of their wedding. Elizabeth was upstairs dressing, she was so nervous, when Rose came in. "I brought you these blue flowers from the garden and a penny for your shoe. Mom thought you might like to barrow something from her." She said as she handed Lizzy a silver comb for her hair.

"Oh, thank you. It is so sweet of you two. These things will make today perfect."

"Are you ready?" Rose inquired as she looked at her watch.

"Yes," Lizzy said with a smile.

The wedding was beautiful. Sweet and simple, just the way Frank and Elizabeth wanted it. It was in the garden with Frank's mom and sister and the minister. After the ceremony was over they had a nice lunch with champagne and wedding cake for desert. Rose stayed to clean up and take care of mom's needs so that Frank and Elizabeth were free to have the rest of the day and evening to themselves. They ended the day with a moonlit walk down by the river.

Frank and Elizabeth took care of Madeline for a year and a half. It was a wonderful time. Frank worked hard at the local ranch. While Elizabeth spent her time cleaning, running errands and taking care of mom. At the end of a year and a half, mom was well and could care for herself. It was time to move on. Frank and Elizabeth were very sad to leave. Elizabeth had grown very close to Madeline.

They moved out and into a four bedroom ranch house on forty acres. It was an old ranch rich in history but somewhat run down. With time, hard work and imagination they would realize their dream.

CHAPTER 7

A year went by. Frank and Elizabeth couldn't have been happier. Their ranch was coming along right on schedule. The cattle prices were up. Every morning they woke up to the most beautiful views, beyond anything Elizabeth had ever imagined.

One evening as they sat eating supper she sat dreamily picking at her food. Seeing how distracted Elizabeth was, Frank inquired, "Lizzy, are you okay?"

A big smile came over her face.

Frank examined her gaze, "What is it?"

Trying to contain her joy and fighting back tears, "We're pregnant!" Elizabeth blurted out.

"We're going to have a baby?! " Frank asked, with shock in his voice.

Elizabeth could only smile and nod.

Frank was very excited. He and Elizabeth sat and let it all sink in.

After supper they left the dishes and the usual evening paperwork and slipped off to bed.

The next morning, while she was in town doing her errands, Elizabeth stopped at the local baby store to look around. She was amazed to find all the neat new baby things they had. Looking in the specialty baby store, she realized how much she had missed by only visiting department stores. What wonderful things they made. They sure made it easier and more convenient than it was when she used to baby-sit.

The next few months raced by. With chores and getting ready for baby, Frank and Elizabeth had little time for anything else. It was a very hectic time. Elizabeth was becoming exhausted as time grew closer.

One day, when Elizabeth was in her seventh month, Frank came to her and said, "You need a break. Go upstairs and put on something nice. Rose and I have a surprise for you."

When Elizabeth returned from dressing she was overcome. Frank and his sister Rose had set up a surprise shower. It was wonderful. Just what she needed. Many of Elizabeth's friends were there. What a surprise, she hadn't seen them since leaving the real estate office. They had shower games and shower prizes. One of the games was to see who could change "the baby" the fastest. (They were donated by some of the ladies daughters.) The prize was a baby bottle filled with candies. The shower lasted four hours.

When it was all over Elizabeth started cleaning up. Frank stopped her. "Rose and I will clean up. It has been a long day for you. You should rest, but first I want to show you my shower gift to you."

She followed him upstairs to the baby's room. Inside was the exact crib Elizabeth had been looking at with matching changing table, dresser and shelves. She was so excited! "But are you sure we can afford this?"

"Did you really think I was fishing every evening for the last week?" Frank said sarcastically.

"I did. I thought with the baby coming you had a lot to think over. I thought you needed some time alone."

Frank smiled. He knew his wife had a caring and loving spirit. It was nice to be reminded just how much, once in a while. "I was out doing odd jobs around town to pay for all this."

They had such a special relationship. That was, they didn't need to say another word. Their love was deeper and stronger than words could ever convey.

CHAPTER 8

Soon time came to go to the hospital. Elizabeth was all packed, ready and waiting. Frank was out punching cows. One of the boys rode out to get him.

Frank was more nervous than he had ever been. It wasn't his first, but he was nervous just the same. He held it together until the nurse said, "Do you want to hold your daughter?"

Frank and Elizabeth decided to name their new addition Sabrina. Looking at her bright new face, Frank knew he had finally found his happiness again. Elizabeth was bursting with joy. She knew a wonderful husband, a new daughter and their ranch in the mountains made her life complete.

The next six months went by better than they could have ever imagined. What a happy baby. Sabrina only cried if she needed something. Most of the time she was all smiles and laughter. By the time Sabrina was six months old she was sleeping through the night and eating on a regular schedule. Frank and Elizabeth decided it was time to allow Sabrina to spend the night at grandma's house. They spent a perfectly romantic evening together. The next morning they awoke to the phone ringing. A sergeant on the other end of the line informed Frank his ex-wife had been found dead in her home.

"Where are the kids? Are they okay? What happened?" He was clearly shaken and upset.

"The children were out when it happened. As for the circumstances, they are still under investigation." Replied the sergeant. "As for the children, they are with child protective services. We would like to get them to you as soon as we can."

Frank was full of emotions. So many thoughts were running through his head.

"Sir… sir, are you still there?"

"I'm sorry. It's a lot to take in right now. Would you like me to come and pick them up?"

"That won't be necessary. We will bring them right out."

"Thank you." Frank said as he hung up the phone.

Elizabeth had been quietly listening to Frank's side of the conversation. "What on earth is going on?!"

He began slowly explaining, "Honey, something horrible has happened." Frank was trying to absorb things as he rehashed his conversation with the sergeant. "Sarah was found dead."

"What?" Elizabeth interrupted. "What about your children. Are they okay?"

"They are safe. An officer will bring them by soon."

"Frank, are you okay?"

"Yes, I just need a minute to take it all in."

Elizabeth's mind was racing. She had always hoped Frank could be in his children's lives again, but not like this. Inside she was very anxious, thoughts kept running through her head. "Okay," Elizabeth took a deep breath and slowly exhaled, "First things first. I'll get dressed and make breakfast. These children are probably tired and hungry. They've had a very long night."

As Frank sat dazed, Elizabeth quickly dressed. "I'll go make some breakfast. Let me know if you need anything." She kissed him and went down stairs.

As he dressed, Frank continued thinking. "He hadn't seen his children in a very long time. How would they feel about him? Would they want to live with him?" Frank looked down at his watch and realized they would be there any minute.

Just as he was tying his last shoe, the doorbell rang. Frank ran down the stairs, stole a kiss as he passed Elizabeth in the kitchen, and arrived at the front door before it rang a second time.

The door opened and there stood his two beautiful children. After two or three minutes of uncomfortable silence, Frank's daughter Phyllis, grabbed him in a great big hug. She sobbed. "Oh daddy, oh daddy…" They just stood there for the next few moments.

Frank looked up from their embrace and saw John. He held Phyllis and took John by the hand. "Come on in." They all walked into the living room.

"I can see things here will okay." Commented the officer. "Someone will be calling on you tomorrow to talk over the legal formalities and to make sure everything is working out okay."

"Thank you. Would you like some coffee?" Frank asked while still holding his children.

"No, thank you." Said the officer as he turned to leave.

"Thank for bringing my children to me." Frank said.

The officer smiled and nodded as he walked out the door.

Hearing the officer leave, and after giving them ten or fifteen minutes alone together, Elizabeth popped out of the kitchen. "Hello." She said cautiously.

"This is Elizabeth … my wife." Frank said.

"Hello." Phyllis and John said together. They were too tired and shaken from the evening's events to give Elizabeth much notice.

"It is very nice to meet you. I am very sorry, but I have an errand to run. I will be back in an hour or so. Breakfast is in the kitchen, if anyone is hungry." Elizabeth leaned over and gave Frank a kiss, "Call me if you need anything."

Elizabeth wanted to leave as soon as possible without being rude. She knew she would be in the way, and Frank and his children would have a lot to talk about.

Soon as she left, they went into the kitchen to eat breakfast. The next half hour or so went on very quietly. Frank and his children were all lost in their own thoughts:

Frank was thinking, "How can we put our relationships back together? Will I be able to help them get past their mother's death? What were they like now as compared to how they were when he last saw them? Will they like it here with us and their new sister?" Frank tried to reassure himself that it would all work out. "I know too much time has passed without any contact, but after all, they were still *his* babies.

John was thinking. "What am I going to do? My mom is gone. I had to move away from all my friends. I'm happy dad was willing to take us in, but why did he leave us like he did? What will Elizabeth be like? Will we have to call her mom? I won't!"

Phyllis was thinking. "Why is life so hard? Mom is gone. Now we are here with dad and *his* new wife. Why did he have to get married again? Maybe I won't have to talk to her much. I won't talk to her unless I have too! She cooks pretty good and seems to take decent care of dad. I am happy to have daddy, but I am scared. I want my mom back!"

Frank interrupted the silence, "Would anyone like a tour of the house?"

"Sure," John and Phyllis shrugged.

After the breakfast dishes were put away, they started on the tour.

"I'm not sure about sleeping arrangements, but as soon as Elizabeth gets back we'll work it out." They walked through the house going from room to room. "This is our room. Here is a bathroom. You can put your dirty things in the hamper. Here are the towels and wash clothes." Then they continued the tour. Soon they came to Sabrina's room. "This is your sister's room." Frank just stood there waiting for their reaction.

Phyllis and John were speechless. After a long pause, Phyllis began slowly. "No one told us. How old is she?"

"She is six months old." Frank replied.

"What's her name?" John asked.

"Her name is Sabrina. Elizabeth went to pick her up from your grandma's house. This was her first night away from home. It's always hard when you are separated, for any amount of time, from your children. No matter how old they are." Frank waited and hoped what he was trying to say sunk in.

After a few minutes, Frank began again. "By the way, when you are ready, we'll have your grandma and aunt over for dinner. They have missed you so much!" Frank had been trying hard not to break down and over whelm the children, but he couldn't hold back any longer. "I've missed you so much! A day hasn't gone by that I haven't thought of you." The tears came pouring out. Then all three of them were crying. It had been a very long night for the children and morning had only brought more changes.

Just about lunch time the phone rang. It was Elizabeth. She had been visiting with Frank's mom and wanted to know if it was time to come home. Frank said it would be a good time. "The kids saw Sabrina's room and are anxious to meet her." He told her as he hung up the phone.

Soon Elizabeth was knocking on the front door. Frank opened it. "Here, will you please take Sabrina?" Her hands were full of the baby and baby things.

As the evening progressed, John and Phyllis met Sabrina, and got to know her. Frank got some temporary beds set up in the den. While Elizabeth ordered a pizza for them. The family finished the evening with a relaxing movie. It was nice to get used to being around each other without the pressure of trying to make conversation.

The next week was full of emotional ups and downs. Everyone was adjusting to life as a new family. John and Phyllis were learning to live life without their mother, but were happy to be back with their father. Elizabeth saw how well they all got along and was very happy to see it. She was having a hard time adjusting to the sudden shift in Frank's attention. Where before his attention was focused on her and Sabrina, now it was mostly on John and Phyllis. Elizabeth was not jealous. She understood they needed a lot right now, but missed her quiet time with Frank.

CHAPTER 9

John and Phyllis were given everything they needed from Frank and Elizabeth. They were beginning to think of Elizabeth as more than just 'The woman their father married'. Things were just beginning to feel put together and comfortable, when new problems arose.

One night, as Elizabeth was in the baby's room putting Sabrina to bed, there was a knock at the door. Frank and John were out in the shop working on one of their many airplanes.

"Phyllis," Elizabeth called.

"Yes?"

"Would you rock the baby awhile? Someone's at the door."

"Okay." It was a pleasure for Phyllis. She and Sabrina had grown very close to each other.

As soon as Elizabeth opened the door she saw two police men, it was very disconcerting to her.

"Hello, may I help you?" Elizabeth asked.

"Is your husband at home? We would like to speak to him." One of the officers asked.

"Yes. Just a moment I will get him. Would you like to come in and wait?"

"Thank you."

Elizabeth left the officers and went out to the shop. "Honey, there's someone at the door for you." She didn't want to worry John. Frank could tell by her expression not to ask questions.

The policemen told Frank they were investigating his ex-wife, Sarah's, murder. They were there to inform him he was a suspect. Tomorrow, they added, Frank should go down to the police station to answer some questions and make a formal statement. Frank said he would and thanked the officers for the information.

Frank figured he would go make a statement and answer some questions and that would be the end of it. But Frank was wrong. In the weeks to come he would find out just how wrong he was.

The next day Frank arrived early at the police station. They asked him many questions. From relevant ones like: Where were you the night your ex-wife was murdered? Did you murder her? How was she killed? Why did you leave her? To not so relevant ones like: What do you like to eat? Are you left or right handed? Do you drink coffee? Of course, what didn't feel relevant to Frank, was relevant to the investigation.

When all of the questions were answered and his statement was taken, Frank went home. After four hours at the police station!

Soon as he drove up, Elizabeth came running out and put her arms around him. She didn't ask any questions, they weren't needed. Frank could see her concern and total support in her eyes. They almost always communicated better without talking. Her only words were, "I love you." Frank slipped his arm around her waist as they walked into the house together.

Frank was happy she didn't ask any questions. He would tell her, but later, when everything was quiet and he had time to think. The children didn't ask anything either. Maybe it was because they could sense it didn't go well, or maybe they really didn't want to know.

Soon after, Frank noticed people were acting differently towards him. It wasn't very noticeable at first. Every day, it seemed people were more and more distant. When Frank went into the town he would hear people talking, but as soon as they noticed Frank or his family, everyone became quiet.

Frank and Elizabeth weren't really sure what was happening until Elizabeth got a call. It was an investigator from the police department. He called to ask her questions about Frank. They were very direct and told her that Frank was their prime suspect. It was very upsetting to her. Every time they turned around (it seemed) Frank and Elizabeth would find another place the police had delved into their lives. Their bank accounts, special funds Frank and Elizabeth had set up for all three children, their safety deposit boxes, and all their financial ventures were investigated. When all the interviews and evidence gathering was almost complete, the police had one more place to look, Frank's house.

Weeks upon weeks passed as Frank's life was brought out in the public eye. It made life very hard for Frank and his family. The police spoke to everyone, dug up old mistakes, old girlfriends, old enemies and brought out other embarrassing things about Frank and other people close to him. The worst day came when the police visited them once again.

Elizabeth answered a knock at the door. "Ma'am, we would like to speak to your husband. Is he at home?" A policeman asked as he stood next to his partner.

"Yes, just a moment. You may wait inside." She said, excusing herself from the room.

"More questions? I thought they were done with us." Elizabeth thought to herself. She was getting more than frustrated with the whole situation.

"Frank, the police are at the front door, again." She said with a sigh.

"Okay, please tell them I will be right down." Frank was so tired of seeing people in uniform. He knew they were only doing their job, but hoped it would be over soon.

As Elizabeth headed down stairs something was different. She had a horrible feeling in the pit of her stomach.

"He'll be right down." She said, looking at the officers, who seemed uneasy. "Can I get you something?"

"No, thank you."

Just as Elizabeth was about to make small talk Frank appeared at the top of the stairs. "Hi fellas! More questions?"

"Yes." one of the officers said. "But these questions will have to be answered down at the station."

The next thing they said didn't register right away. It was as if Frank and Elizabeth were in a fog, one that was suffocating. "We are placing you under arrest for the murder of your ex-wife, Sarah." As the officers continued, Frank hugged and kissed his wife. Then he was placed in hand cuffs and lead out to the police car.

"I'll call your lawyer, make arrangements for the kids and be down as soon as I can." Elizabeth was scared, confused and very angry.

CHAPTER 10

Down at the station Frank had time to reflect on the previous weeks, he had been very cooperative during the investigation, and now he was beside himself with anger. They processed him and put him in a room to question him.

"I hope this means I'll get some answers," thought Frank. But he didn't, instead he was given a grueling two hour interview. Questions like: 'Where were you the night of Sarah's murder?' and 'What were her reasons for leaving you?' So many questions, accusations. They brought up things that had nothing to do with motive or the actual night she was murdered. Frank was confused, tired and ready to just give up. But instead of giving into their questions, he waited for his attorney.

It was quite a wait, but they finally let up long enough for Frank to have some coffee and rest. It was a good thing he did, because as soon as his attorney showed up, the questions started all over again. Frank was advised to give a statement with his whereabouts on the night in question. After that, his attorney advised him to not answer any more questions.

Frank told his attorney to advise Elizabeth to stay at home, and come down in the morning after the children go to school.

That night Frank slept in a jail cell wondering what would happen next. His night was anything but restful. There were unfamiliar noises all around him and he was alone with his own thoughts and fears. As much as he wanted sleep to come, it wouldn't.

Not sleeping well herself, she was up and dressed before the rooster could cock-a-doodle-do. She went down stairs and began setting things up for breakfast. Elizabeth wanted to make things easier for the children. It was promising to be a long day for all of them. Phyllis and John emerged from their bedrooms yawning and stretching, it had been a long night for them too. Elizabeth explained that she was going down to the station to talk to their father and find out if there was a way to bring him home. Soon as the kids were off to school, Elizabeth left to take Sabrina to Grandma's, and head to the station.

Down at the station, she waited and waited. Finally they allowed Elizabeth in to see Frank. He looked like he was rode hard and put up wet. Elizabeth wasn't allowed to see him very long, but she was able to find out some things that she could do to make his stay a little easier. In the meantime, Frank's attorney promised to keep her apprised of everything that was happening.

On the way home, Elizabeth tried to figure out the best way to talk to the children. "They have been through so much, now this." She often voiced her private thoughts while driving alone in her car. "What possible evidence could they have?" She was so stressed and confused, Elizabeth couldn't think about it any longer. With the radio blaring, she drove home to her next challenge, helping the children through this mess.

When Elizabeth walked through the door she was greeted by John. "Hi, Lizzy." The children had begun to call her by her nickname, and she really liked it. She finally felt as though they had accepted her.

"Where's dad?"

"I wasn't able to bring him home...They booked him on a murder charge." Elizabeth wasn't sure how to put it, but up front and honest was the only way she knew how. "They...think...he killed your mother." The words came out hard. She waited for them to sink in.

After a long pause, John began, but slowly. "Do you think there is any possibility?!" He was shocked and very confused.

This question upset Elizabeth, but she set her anger aside. After all it was a fair question, John had not seen his father in many years. He didn't really know Frank.

"No, there isn't any possibility. Your father was angry for the way things turned out with your mother and not being able to see you children. But he'd never do anything to hurt your mother."

"I'm sorry. I know he didn't. I just had to ask. What do we do now?"

"I don't really think we can do much more than wait and see. I wish there were. If we can keep things together and going here it will help your father's emotional state. Let's start with that." Elizabeth patted John's back. She wanted to give him a reassuring hug, but like his father, he wasn't 'a touchy feely kind of guy' (as Frank put it).

"Is your sister home from school?"

"She is upstairs trying to concentrate on her studies."

Just then Phyllis came down. "How did it go?" She inquired, as she desperately searched their faces for possible answers, John spoke to her. "They kept dad and booked him for murder. They think *he* killed mom." Phyllis was so shocked the words barely registered.

As John heard himself say these words, he could hardly contain his anger. He bolted out the door, letting it slam behind him. Soon as John was outside he yelled as loud as he could. Collapsing to the ground! With tears streaming down his face, he lay there sobbing.

Phyllis too, was overwhelmed. She and Elizabeth held onto each other and cried and cried. When everyone was calmer, Elizabeth left to pick up Sabrina and some take-out. Soon as they were home the family decided no one was going anywhere else today, and Elizabeth would call the children in sick tomorrow.

CHAPTER 11

After a week in jail, Frank found himself in front of a judge. "What is your plea, young man?"

"Not guilty, your honor." Frank was very quiet, polite and to the point. He had been very cooperative and truthful while in police custody. This seemed to impress the judge. As the attorneys finished their arguments, the judge made his decision. He let Frank out on bail. The bail was set high because the charge was murder. Frank and Elizabeth decided they had to take a second mortgage on their ranch.

That evening, after Sabrina was put to bed, Frank asked to talk to the family. He told Elizabeth, John and Phyllis what he found out while in jail. "The police told me they had an eye witness, who said they saw me leave the house and run off down the street."

"Who was this eye witness?" Elizabeth inquired.

"They wouldn't divulge that sort information." Frank was very frustrated with the police department.

Phyllis and John sat listening to their father and stepmother talking over what had happened they were worried what might happen next. Finally, Phyllis spoke up, "I'm sorry, but I can't sit here and relive the events surrounding mom's murder. I'm going up to my room." Phyllis walked quickly to her room, noticeably shaken.

"Me too." John added, "This is too much."

Frank's heart sank. He hadn't thought about them and how this related to the loss of their mother. He was upset with himself! Elizabeth felt bad too, but she had it together enough to realize that the children could probably use a little distraction from their thoughts. "Frank may we finish this discussion later this evening?"

He could see what Lizzy was up to. "Of course, what's up?" Frank said with a grin.

"How about we order some pizza, pop some popcorn and get a movie?" Lizzy hardly ever let them have a drink in the living room. Pizza, now this was a first! The children were very pleased to have a break from all the stress. It felt, at least at that moment, that things were normal and comfortable.

Later that evening, when the kids were tucked in bed, Frank and Elizabeth finished their conversation. "I am going to find out who killed her. If I don't they will put me in prison." Frank said with a ragged sigh.

"Isn't that dangerous? Are you sure you can't trust the police to do their job? What about your attorney?" Elizabeth was acting irrational. Saying things as quickly as they entered her mind was not like her, but she was scared. The most she had ever been in her entire life.

Frank gently took her by the shoulders and looked her in the eye. With a firm but gentle tone, he said, "My attorney can only do so much. The evidence is stacked against me. What *are* the police to think? If I leave it up to other people, I am afraid, I will end up in hot water. I won't risk what we have, and if I am convicted I could get the death penalty. I have to try and clear myself. I don't have another choice."

At this point Frank had his arms around Elizabeth, she was starting to cry. Trying to hold back her tears. "What can I do to help?" Elizabeth was not all comfortable with Frank's plan but she had complete faith in Frank.

"I'll let you know. I have some things to look into, but you keeping things in order here will allow me to concentrate on the things I need to do. We ought to get some sleep. I'll go into town tomorrow and talk to some people that might be able to help or give me some information. I want you to know, Lizzy… I couldn't have gotten this far without you."

Elizabeth just smiled. She laid there for a long time snuggled in Frank's arms just listening to him sleep. She cherished every moment so much more knowing they may lose these special times. It was scary to think what it would be like not to see him every day. Then Elizabeth started thinking about Frank locked away in a cage. They lived in the country for many reasons, one being open spaces, no confinement! What would he do? Elizabeth went to sleep feeling scared, angry and confused.

The alarm was set for five a.m., as usual, but she was up at three. Elizabeth tried to be quiet, but could tell Frank was being disturbed. She couldn't escape her thoughts from the night before, so decided to go downstairs to make some coffee. About a half an hour later Lizzy was joined by Phyllis.

"Good morning, you're up early. Didn't you sleep well?" Elizabeth inquired.

"Oh, okay, I guess. I'm worried about dad. I don't think things look very good for him. What will happen if they say he did it?" Phyllis was very nervous.

Elizabeth tried to console Phyllis. "No matter what happens, we are a family and we will stick together. If the worst happens, we can run this ranch until your father returns. I know I am not your mother, but no matter what, I will always be here for you and your brother."

"It makes me feel better to hear you say that. I know you will be, but I really needed to hear it from you." Phyllis said smiling through her tears.

It was nice to have this time together. They hardly ever talked, especially about important or emotional issues. Phyllis was an introvert. It was very hard for her to let anyone in. To see the real person, inside.

Now, from their conversation, Elizabeth felt closer to Phyllis than she had ever felt before. When Phyllis first came to live with them she hardly spoke to anyone. Everyone understood. Her life had just been turned upside down, but it had been a long time between then and now. Her progress was very slow.

Elizabeth was afraid Phyllis would slip backwards with her father being accused of her mother's brutal murder. This little conversation made Elizabeth feel like Phyllis had a chance of making it through all of this, and maybe she could help her along the way. Elizabeth reached over and gave Phyllis a hug. They both needed one.

Just then Frank walked in. He walked over and joined the embrace. Soon after, John walked in. No one said a thing. All four of them stood there in a long overdue group hug, as a family. As they separated the silence continued.

"What's for breakfast?" Frank asked, to break it.

"How does bacon, eggs and toast sound?" Was Elizabeth's reply.

Everyone made breakfast and cleaned up together. Taking time to enjoy each other's company. They all knew how precious their time would be over the next few weeks and how little of it they would have.

CHAPTER 12

Today Frank would start his own investigation into his ex-wife's murder. The trick was not getting caught in a position that looks to the police that he is trying to conceal evidence.

Frank sat down with Phyllis and John. He didn't want to involve them but he needed the information. It had been so long since he knew anything about his ex-wife, Sarah. Frank didn't want to know, but there was no other way to clear himself.

"I only need to know what was going on in the past couple of years. I may need more information later. For now we can start with closer to the present." Frank wasn't sure what to say or how to talk to them about this.

The kids seemed pretty at ease (for what they were talking about). Elizabeth sat between Phyllis and John on the couch. Sabrina was playing in her playpen. This helped give distraction when the questions got a little hard to bare.

Frank decided to start with the most traumatic part, the night of the murder. If they could get past this part the rest would be a lot easier.

Phyllis started, "We weren't home when it happened. I don't know what we can tell you."

"What happened when you came home?" Frank asked, hoping to get them talking.

The children looked at him trying to figure out what they could say that might help.

"This isn't working," thought Frank. He sat there thinking, getting more and more frustrated as the clock ticked on. "Let's try something else," he suggested. "Was your mother...did she...was she dating?" Frank felt very awkward, but had to ask.

"A couple of times I heard mom talking to a guy on the phone, but I never knew his name. Mom and I didn't talk about her friends." John's voice trailed off. He and his mother had a typical mother teen age son relationship. They only talked about things that didn't have an emotional attachment for either of them.

Phyllis sat quietly listening to find out what John knew. She was uncomfortable and it showed. Elizabeth sensed something that no one else did. "Can we take a break?" She suggested. Frank started to disagree, but Elizabeth gave him a knowing glance, which changed his mind.

Elizabeth asked Phyllis to join her in the kitchen. "Would you like some tea?"

Phyllis nodded and seemed to relax a bit.

"This isn't easy for you, is it?"

"My mom and I talked about everything... Even her...her and dad." Her voice trailed off. Just then the tea pot started to whistle.

After the tea was poured they relaxed and sipped some of their tea. Then Elizabeth began. "It's okay to have feelings. No matter what you feel. Or how others perceive your feelings. They are yours, and it's okay." She paused to let her words sink in. "I know you loved your mother. I know you love your father. I understand it is very hard to tell your mother's personal life, especially to your father, but he needs to hear it right now. Believe it or not, it is just as hard for him to hear it. Even after all your mother and he went through he still has a small place where he carries love for her." Elizabeth stopped to pour Phyllis some more tea. Then she left the kitchen to offer tea or cocoa to the guys, and give Phyllis some time, some space to think.

"How is she doing?" John and Frank were sitting on the couch waiting.

"She'll be okay. Just give her a few minutes more. This is a lot of stress on her." Elizabeth commented.

Frank understood and waited while Lizzy went to check on his daughter. As she left he started thinking, "What a wonderful wife. She is so loving and patient. I hate putting everyone through all this turmoil, no matter how necessary it might be." Soon, he hoped it would all be over.

Finally, emerging from the kitchen, Phyllis began. "It's important to catch the person who did this, so I will help. I'm sorry if any of it hurts you." She was still feeling uneasy. How could she hurt her father so much?

Frank finally understood. His daughter wasn't upset because it was just hurting her, she was worried about hurting him, too.

"Phyllis," Frank started slowly. His voice had gentle, but firm fatherly tones. "When your mother left and took you from me, I was hurt. I have always been angry with her for deciding to take you and John away from me. I have never forgiven her for making things so hard on both of you. She knew I would not make it worse by disrupting your lives. So she took you away. I got over my hurt that was connected to the love your mom and I once shared. Anything you tell me about your mom and her boyfriends won't break my heart. I just want to get past this and keep us together so we may be a family again." He felt as though he was rambling, but hoped Phyllis would understand.

After their talk, Frank and Phyllis felt better, and were able to finish their discussion about Sarah. They taped their conversation so neither one would have to do this again.

* * * * * * * * * * * * * *

Phyllis' mother, Sarah, was very unhappy after the divorce. She regretted what she had done. One morning, while the children were in school, she summoned all her courage and called Frank. Sarah wanted him back.

Before the phone call Frank was able to talk to his children whenever he wanted. He was also able to see them, with limited access. Sarah made sure she was always in control.

When Frank answered the phone he was surprised to hear her voice. She explained how she missed him and wanted to try again. He thought for a moment. Frank realized right then and there how much control she wanted over him. How often had she played with his heart and easy going nature? How rough would it be on the children the next time she got angry and kicked him out?

Frank told Sarah, "No."

Because of her vindictive nature, Sarah decided if she couldn't have him, he would never see his children again.

Sarah never got over Frank. She had many boyfriends, but nothing too serious. In her eyes, no one could ever measure up to Frank.

Phyllis told Frank, "When mom…died, she was dating two men. One of them was named Jay Jacobson. He was a police officer. Mr. Jacobson was nice, but was very quiet around John and me. I think he was a shy sort of person. That's all I really know about him."

"The only other man was in the military. He wasn't around much. He was direct and stiff as a tree. I was very uncomfortable around him. His name was Lt. Jorgensen. I never heard his first name. He always seemed like John and I were in the way." Phyllis gave all the information that she could to her father. She hoped it was enough to help.

CHAPTER 13

The next morning Frank woke up bright and early to hunt for clues. He decided to talk to some of the neighbors. Most gave little to no information. Feeling down and very frustrated, Frank continued on to Mrs. Baker's house. He found she was one of the sweetest neighbors. Mrs. Baker had a lot of information and was very willing to help Frank.

She was having trouble sleeping that night. The strange thing was she didn't hear anything. Sarah had a dog that always barked at strangers. Not that night and the dog was not harmed.

Earlier in the evening an unmarked police car was parked a coupled of houses down from Sarah's. The next morning, when Mrs. Baker went out to pick up her paper, she noticed the car was gone.

After further discussion, Mrs. Baker remembered seeing a light on in Sarah's room at 12:36 am. She remembered the time because the movie she was watching had just ended. When she got up to close her shades the light from Sarah's room caught her attention.

Frank thanked Mrs. Baker for the information. "Maybe you can come by to visit. The kids would love to see you, and you can meet my wife and daughter."

Mrs. Baker smiled and agreed to come by someday soon.

Mrs. Baker had been very helpful. She brought up many new and unanswered questions. Frank got home as quickly as he could. Soon as he walked in the door Lizzy came rushing up to give him a hug and kiss.

"What was that for?" Asked a startled Frank.

Lizzy just stood there smiling. "I just missed you, and wanted you to know it."

Frank looked at her with a puzzled expression. His eyes said, "What is really going on here?"

Lizzy just said, "Baby."

Frank stood there with information overload. He was trying to process his conversation with Mrs. Baker, and figure out his next step. Now he finds out there is another baby on the way.

Elizabeth and Frank walked into the living room to sit down. After a long silence Frank was ready to talk. "Honey, that's wonderful! Do you have any idea when?"

"About nine months from last week, I think. I will go to the doctor in a few days. Then we will have a better idea.

How did your interviews go?"

"It went well. I met Mrs. Baker. She is a sweet lady. Just like the kids' said. She sure missed John and Phyllis." Frank continued telling Elizabeth all the facts he got from Mrs. Baker. When he finished he asked Elizabeth if she could find a way to get the police report without anyone getting suspicious. She said she would try.

* * * * * * * * * * * * *

The next morning Elizabeth left the house very early. When she was gathering her things to go out, Frank saw her and asked where she was going. Elizabeth only said she would be back later with the police report. Then she left.

Frank got up and started catching up on his outside work. He always thought better when he was breaking a sweat. An hour or so later Phyllis emerged from the house with Sabrina. "Dad, I have a phone call. Would you please take her for a while?"

Frank was happy for a break. While Phyllis was busy he played with Sabrina. He missed their father daughter time. Sabrina was growing so fast, it felt like ages since they had played together.

Elizabeth got home to find Phyllis busy with household chores. Frank was outside happily playing with Sabrina. John was in his room working on a school project. She stood at the bottom of the stairs drinking in the serenity of the moment. "Hi sweetie." Elizabeth smiled warmly. "I have the report for you."

"Wonderful! How did you manage it?"

"My womanly charms." She said raising her eyebrows.

Frank laughed. "Have you had lunch?"

Elizabeth was famished. Frank decided to take everyone out to lunch. It was a good day. One that felt somewhat normal.

That night when all was quiet, and everyone else was asleep, Frank sat alone reviewing his life. It was a good life, full of adventure, sorrow and pain. These years with Lizzy felt homey and he finally felt understood and loved for who he was. He went to bed feeling content and happy. Knowing that whatever might come. Elizabeth will always love him.

CHAPTER 14

Things were rapidly changing. Frank, John and Phyllis had found the family bond they thought had been lost. Elizabeth and Sabrina were accepted and growing very close to John and Phyllis. Now there was a new member, of their ever growing family, coming soon. The police investigation was in full swing and so was Frank's.

Now that he had the police report in his hands, he felt he was finally getting somewhere. It was packed with more information than Frank had imagined. It told of the two men, a Jay Jacobson and a Lt. Jorgenson. Sarah was dating them both when she was murdered.

Mr. Jacobson was a police officer from two towns over. He and Sarah met one afternoon at the county fair. They hit it off, right away. And were seeing a lot of each other, until their meetings started slowing down.

It seemed about the time things started slowing down people started seeing Sarah with a new man. His name was Lt. Jorgenson. He was in the marines. It didn't say, in the police report, how they met. But it did tell the names of the people interviewed. Frank decided he would interview the same people the police did. Maybe he could get more detailed information. Some of them might feel more comfortable talking to him, rather than the police. Frank also had the kids to clarify some of the information for him.

Over the course of the next few weeks, Frank conducted many interviews and gathered many more facts. The children were weathering the new questions well. They weren't able to provide much new information, but the few answers they provided helped quite a bit.

As usual, Elizabeth made sure the household ran smoothly and the children were well cared for.

Frank ran into a few close-calls with the police. They didn't like that he was interfering in a police investigation. Twice he was almost put back in jail.

When the long weeks were over, Frank sat down with Elizabeth to review all the facts he had collected. Maybe they could decipher who it was, with enough proof to dismiss Frank as a suspect and put the killer in jail.

Frank decided to list out the main points to make it easier to sort through the facts:

Fact one: Sarah was dating two men when she was murdered.

A. One was a police officer named Jay Jacobson.

B. One was a military officer named Lt. Jorgenson.

Fact two: Lt. Jorgenson was married.

A. Sarah didn't know, but she started suspecting he had another girlfriend.

    1. He only gave her his cell number.

    2. Wouldn't tell her where he lived.

    3. Was very secretive about his home life.

    4. Anytime she wanted to go out he had an excuse to stay in.

CHAPTER 15

While Frank was gathering information he began to notice a lot of unmarked police cars. He started feeling a bit paranoid. As the days went by Elizabeth found there seemed to be a large police presence around the house. The kids came home feeling as though someone was watching them. Frank decided they needed to know what was going on. Who was following and keeping tabs on all of them.

Elizabeth called the police department to report a suspicious person parked down the street. The police told her they would check it out. Ten minutes later, a patrol car came and spoke to the person down the street. Then the policemen came to Elizabeth's door. Instead of telling her who was down the street, they asked for Frank.

"He isn't here," answered Elizabeth.

"What has he been up to lately?" One of the officers asked, sternly.

"I don't know what you are trying to imply." Elizabeth was angry and at the end of her rope, so she came off angry and defensive. It was not the way she wanted to present herself to them. Up to now she was kind and seemingly helpful, but now she realized they were effecting the children's day to day lives. "Frank has been working and hanging out at home with his family."

"Give him a message: Tell him to review the conditions of his bail. Unless, he wants to go back to jail before his trial date."

"Yes sir! I'll give him the message." At this point it was very apparent why everyone was feeling watched lately. "Please give whomever is in charge a message for me: Tell him to review the laws concerning police harassment, and leave Frank's children alone, they've been through enough!"

With that they left in a huff.

When Frank returned home Elizabeth filled him in with the day's events.

"I may have overreacted, but I am so sick of arrogant people. How dare they, cause these children anymore disruption in their somewhat normal lives?!" Elizabeth was fuming. It took a lot to get her this angry and when she was, it took her along time to calm down.

Frank sat calmly allowing her to rant and rave. When she was finished, she was crying. Elizabeth walked over and sat next to Frank. He just sat and held her. When she was through Frank got up and paced the floor. It was hard putting his family through all of this, but it would come to an end someday. Then they would all get on with their lives. Hopefully 'someday' would come soon.

Frank went to bed early that night. He was exhausted, but couldn't sleep. After a long night of tossing and turning, it was time to gather all the information he'd collected. He had wanted to take it to the police, but first he had a lot of sifting to do.

Elizabeth woke up very early. Frank was in the den. "Good morning sweetheart." She said with a worried expression. "Would you like some coffee?"

Frank barely looked up from his piles of papers and pictures. "Yes," was all he said. He looked exhausted!

Elizabeth went into the kitchen. She could tell this wasn't the time to bother him with concerns about his sleep or lack of it. Frank was on a mission, one that wouldn't be interrupted. Even by a loving concerned wife.

Soon, Elizabeth, returned with coffee. She made it just the way Frank liked it. The steamy cup was so hot she almost dropped it on the desk! "Sorry, dear."

"It's okay. Are you all right?"

"Yes. It was just hot." She paused a moment, watching him go over the stack of papers on his desk. "I love you. Let me know if I can help, or if you need anything." Elizabeth gave Frank a peck and a worried smile as she left the room.

Frank knew she was concerned and wanted to say so. But, she understood he was wrapped up in things. Knowing how much she cared and loved him made his job easier.

Frank began feeling overwhelmed by all the evidence. He still didn't have the killer. He needed help from someone with resources he didn't have.

"Lizzy…" Frank called. "Do you know where Hunter's number is?"

"Who?"

"Hunter O'Conner, the police officer."

"I wrote it in your book." She said as she entered the room. Elizabeth carried Frank's address book with her. "What are you calling him for? If the police find out you've violated your bail agreement, they'll put you into jail."

"Don't worry dear. You know Hunter, he's my friend. He'll give me good advice. I won't tell him everything until I know I can still trust him."

When Frank was a youngster he tried to be the kind of child his parents wanted him to be, but he grew up in a rough neighborhood. There came a time in his teens where he felt he had to prove himself. Some older boys talked him into being the look out during a beer robbery. In the end, Frank got arrested, and the other boys got away. The arresting officer was Hunter O'Conner.

Officer O'Conner talked with Frank and decided he wasn't a bad kid. He began mentoring Frank. As his mentor they spent a lot of time together. Officer O'Conner got him involved in a local horse camp. It kept him out of trouble and gave him an outlet for his frustrations.

At the camp Frank worked long hard hours. He was exhausted at the end of each day, but it was worth it. With his experience, Frank was able to do ranch work as he grew. He fell in love with the land and grew a deep respect for the creatures that roamed it.

Frank got a hold of Officer O'Conner. He explained to him he was in a fix and would like to speak with him. Officer O'Conner agreed to meet with Frank at his house. He felt he could give Frank some direction.

The next day Officer O'Conner and Frank sat down over a cup of coffee and some of Elizabeth's homemade danishes, to discuss Frank's dilemma. As Frank spoke, Hunter sat thoughtfully listening to him. He waited for Frank to finish. Then sat there mulling it over.

Finally, after a long silence, he spoke. "Frank, you are in quite a mess. Why, even recruiting me in this matter, could get you put in jail. I could get fired if they knew you were talking to me and I didn't report it. Why should I take a chance on that?"

"Because I am innocent." Was all Frank said.

Hunter knew his friend. Most of what was needed to be said wasn't said with words. Frank needed help and Hunter was the only one that could do it. He agreed to help Frank, but it would be a great risk, for both of them.

Hunter had a friend in another precinct that could get information without a lot of questions or inquires. Soon he had a copy of the police report, complete with names and interviews from the investigation. It was more recent and much more complete than the one Elizabeth acquired.

Two days later Officer Hunter O'Conner, was sitting in Frank's kitchen. They sat mapping out all the information from the two reports and Frank's own investigation.

Looking at Hunter's report first: Mrs. Jones was found dead in the upstairs bedroom. No sign of burglary. She was beaten, stabbed several times, and then strangled. No sign of sexual assault. The murder was very brutal. There was forced entry in through the kitchen door in the rear of the residence.

There was a dog present in the rear yard. Neighbors did not hear the dog barking. The dog always barked at strangers or unfamiliar people. There was no sign of drugs in the dog's system. Neither was he gagged or altered in anyway.

The night of the murder a witness just finished a movie and noticed a light on in the bedroom. It was approximately 12:36 am.

On the same evening there was an unmarked police car parked down the street. The witness checked in the morning and found the car was gone.

One person of interest was a boyfriend. He was a police officer and possibly the one down the street. His name was Jay Jacobson. Hunter checked the reports and didn't find a reason for a police officer in that neighborhood. The report stated that all the officers assigned to that area were not stopped there at that time.

Further on in the report it showed that Mr. Jacobson admitted parking down the road. He said he knew she was dating another man and was not jealous. Mrs. Jones had been acting nervously and he was concerned about her safety.

The second person of interest was a military officer. His name was Lt. Jorgenson. He was married and dating Mrs. Jones when she was murdered. Lt. Jorgenson's wife stated, 'she only found out about the affair when the police came to question her husband.'

Everyone that knew Lt. Jorgenson said he was quiet and a hard ass. Someone that easily unnerved you just by his presence. He was very unpredictable, sometimes volatile. One witness that knew them stated: When Mrs. Jones and Lt. Jorgenson met they were very happy, but that all changed. He became suspicious of almost everything she did. He was possessive and very aggressive. 'It was getting scary.' Lt. Jorgenson wanted to be able call Mrs. Jones day or night and he always checked up on her.

Lt. Jorgenson would not allow Mrs. Jones to call him at home. Things were not making sense to her, so Mrs. Jones called Lt. Jorgenson's house, and soon found out about his marriage. The day after Mrs. Jones was murdered, she was to meet Lt. Jorgenson for lunch. She was going to tell him it was over.

The police questioned her best friend, Ms. Joanne Thatcher. Sarah and Joanne knew each other from high school. About the time Frank and Sarah met they lost touch. It was a busy time for both of them. Joanne was going to college and starting a career. Sarah was starting a family. Soon after her divorce Sarah was lonely and looking for a friend she could count on, so she turned to Joanne. It was a good time for Joanne too. Her career was becoming mundane. Soon they were meeting routinely, every Saturday for lunch, at the same restaurant.

The police checked Sarah's route to and from the restaurant. They also thoroughly investigated the restaurant. For all their efforts, they turned up nothing.

Further on in the report: Ms. Thatcher stated that the day of the murder Mrs. Jones called her sounding very nervous. Mrs. Jones wanted to meet Ms. Thatcher, and stated she was not feeling safe. But Mrs. Jones never made the meeting.

There was an eye witness: A man by the name of Robby Jenkins. He claimed he saw Frank running away from the house on the night of the murder.

The investigating officer concluded that whoever killed Sarah was known to her and the family pet (dog). With the murder being so brutal. It must have been someone very angry with her. Someone that hated her, wanted to terrify her and make her suffer great pain.

With an eye witness and the fact that she took the children away from the ex-husband, the investigator felt Frank was the prime suspect in this case.

The rest of the report gave little helpful information to Frank. He decided he needed to speak to Ms. Thatcher. She, being Sarah's best friend, was someone that would know more than most about her and what was happening around the time of Sarah's death.

He told Hunter what he was planning. Frank wasn't sure if it was a good idea, but Hunter agreed. "You don't have a lot of options right now. Ms. Thatcher might be able to give you an insight no one else can."

The next day Frank went over to Ms. Thatcher's apartment. The evening before he and Elizabeth sat down and went over questions Frank might want to ask.

Hoping for the best, Frank rang the bell. Ms. Thatcher opened the door, looking very surprised. "Hello…you must be Frank. Sarah's ex-husband." She said with a slight tear to her voice.

"Yes I am. I hope I'm not disturbing you."

"No. Please come in."

"If you don't mind my asking, how did you know who I was?" Frank asked. After all, he had never met her before today.

"Sarah was my best friend. We talked about everything. One day she showed me a picture of you. You look the same; just a bit more tired."

"I have been accused of Sarah's murder, so I have come here hoping to add information to my investigation. The police are building a case against me, so I am trying to prove my innocence. Would you be willing to help me?" Frank was nervous. Joanne could call the police anytime and turn him in, if she didn't believe him. It was a chance, but Frank was taking it.

Ms. Joanne Thatcher looked thoughtfully at Frank. "I see," she said slowly, "Of all the things Sarah told me, honesty was very important to you. I don't think you would have taken a chance and come here, if you were guilty. I would like to help. I want to know who…murdered Sarah and see him pay!"

Frank and Ms. Thatcher spoke for hours. She had a lot of information from the many times she and Sarah spent together:

"Sarah was a very sad and confused person. She was a bit obsessive and never got over you, Frank. Taking the kids was her way of getting back at you. If she couldn't control what you did, she would try to control how you felt. Sarah also felt if she had the children you would have to see her. Then she could pretend she wasn't in love with you anymore. I was angry with her for that. It seemed foolish to ruin her life and the children's." Tears were starting to form in her eyes. "I'm sorry. Her whole life after you seemed so wasteful. I wish she could have seen it."

Ms. Thatcher paused. Took a deep breath and started again. "Sarah was seeing two men at the time... When we lost her. One of the men was a police officer by the name of Jay Jacobson. He was very possessive. Officer Jacobson found out about the other boyfriend. He was very jealous and told Sarah he wanted to talk to her." Ms. Thatcher took a deep breath. With a look of concern, continued. "Sarah called me the week before... She told me Jay, I mean Officer Jacobson, called her. They were to meet at a deli downtown, the next day. Sarah asked me if I would go with her. Of course, I said yes... She was really nervous."

"At the deli, I sat at the table next to theirs. Officer Jacobson told Sarah he loved her, but wasn't willing to share her with anyone. He asked, more like begged, Sarah to marry him. She said no. Sarah told him, no one would ever take the place of you, Frank."

Ms. Thatcher looked directly into Frank's eyes. "Frank," she said with a dramatic pause, "You broke Sarah's heart. No one was ever good enough, after you. I know Sarah kicked you out, but it was the biggest mistake of her life!" Looking down with a sigh, "Sadly she would never admit it."

"May we take a break?"

"Of course."

"Would you like some coffee?" Ms. Thatcher asked.

"Yes, thank you." Frank answered.

He needed a break too. All of this was very difficult for Frank. Throughout his investigation, he was forced to relive all his old feelings. This conversation was one of the most difficult. Frank never got completely over Sarah. He knew what she had done and why. Taking the kids was her way of manipulating their situation, and that is why he gave up. Frank wasn't going to allow the kids to become pawns in one of her little game. A long time ago he thought it might have been better for the children, if he went back, but he never would have been able trust her, ever again. That too, he felt, would be hurtful to Phyllis and John. Even with all that had passed in their lives, Frank still loved Sarah. He thought after his all his recent conversations about her, he would have been gotten used to thinking about her and would be able to put all those feelings away. But now they were all coming to the surface, again. And it made listening to Ms. Thatcher talk about Sarah's boyfriends, very difficult.

Soon as Ms. Thatcher came back with their coffee, she started again. "Officer Jacobson scared Sarah. She called me after the meeting at the deli, more scared than ever before."

"The day before her murder, Sarah called me to say, Jay, I mean Officer Jacobson's jealousy was stronger than ever. She was terrified of him. That was the last time I saw or spoke to either one of them." Ms. Thatcher was tearing up.

Frank looked thoughtfully at her. "I know this is hard for you. Would you tell me about Sarah's other boyfriend, or do you want to make it another day?" Frank was hoping she would want to continue. The possibility of the police finding out he was investigating, on his own, was on his mind. A bigger issue, he was becoming emotionally drained, and didn't want to go through this interview again.

Frank breathed a silent breath of relief as Ms. Thatcher chose to continue. He could see she wanted to be done just as much as he did.

"Sarah was seeing another man. His name was Lt. Jorgenson. I met him over at her house. It was kind of strange. I asked Sarah and Lt. Jorgenson if they wanted to go out for dinner. I had heard of a new restaurant in town, and thought it would be fun. Sarah liked the idea, but he said no, absolutely not! It wasn't that he didn't want to go, that was so weird, was the way he reacted to the mere suggestion.

The next day Sarah apologized for the way Lt. Jorgenson had acted. She said he never wanted to go anywhere with her unless it was out of town. Sarah was getting suspicious about him. It was as if he was going out with someone else, and didn't want Sarah to discover it. As far as she was concerned, they were just dating. They weren't exclusive to each other. So it was hard for her to understand why he would react that way. She never remembered giving him any indication that it was more than that."

"Lt. Jorgenson called Sarah a week before her death." Tears began again in Ms. Thatcher's eyes. "Excuse me…I need a minute."

"I understand," Frank said as she got up and went into her room.

Frank looked over his notes to see if he was missing any details to any questions they had already covered. Ms. Thatcher came back in feeling a little better.

"I'm sorry." She apologized.

"Don't be. This is a very difficult thing to talk about." Frank paused. Sympathetically he said, "You and Sarah were obviously very close."

Ms. Thatcher said, "I am ready to tell you the rest. Like I said, Lt. Jorgenson called the week before…Sarah…died." She took a deep breath. "Sarah told me he wanted to talk. She said something in Lt. Jorgenson's voice made her nervous. I asked Sarah if she wanted me to go with her. She said no."

"After their meeting, Sarah called me. She said Lt. Jorgenson was married. He wanted to leave his wife and marry Sarah, but she didn't want to marry him. And now knowing how untrustworthy he was, she decided not to see him anymore." Ms. Thatcher stopped, sighed and looked sadly at Frank. "She wasn't that interested in him anyway. Sarah told him not to call her or come to see her anymore. It was over. Lt. Jorgenson was very upset. Sarah said he understood, and would not bother her anymore. She felt he was being honest."

"That week I called Sarah every day. She seemed to be doing okay, but seemed a little nervous. On the day before her death Sarah seemed anxious. When I called the next morning she didn't answer. I left messages on her home phone and her cell phone. I tried three or four times. I finally reached her about eleven thirty. By then, she was scared. I asked Sarah what was wrong. It was a weird call she got the night before, a threatening call." Ms. Thatcher took a deep breath and thought for a moment. She was trying to remember what Sarah told her the caller had said.

"It was something like: 'We know where you live. You can't have life after you took away hers.'"

"Wait." Frank broke in, "Are you sure Sarah said 'we and hers'?" Frank was hoping this was a break. He desperately needed one.

"Yes, I am sure." Ms. Thatcher said, after much thought.

"I asked Sarah if she would like me to come and stay the night with her. She said no, she would be fine. We made plans to spend the next day together." Ms. Thatcher began to cry. "If only I hadn't listened and gone over to her house that evening."

"Don't worry about what might have been. You had no idea what was going to happen." Frank was trying to show sympathy while containing his excitement. He, finally, had a new lead! "Thank you, Ms. Thatcher. You've helped a lot. I'll let you know what I find out."

"Thank you. By the way, I always knew she was wrong to make you leave. Sarah knew it too, and always regretted it." With that said Ms. Thatcher closed the door. Frank left ready to follow up his new lead.

CHAPTER 16

Elizabeth listened and waited as Frank reviewed his notes, "Whose life could Sarah have ruined?"

"I'm not sure, but I am going to go back over the police reports and my notes. There has to be an answer somewhere!" Frank was sure it was the missing clue.

Elizabeth was in the kitchen making coffee, when Frank came in, looking very tired. "How are you holding up?"

She was happy he was taking a break. This investigation was taking a toll on him. But Elizabeth knew he would not rest until the mystery was solved and he was cleared. Frank had to. For himself and Elizabeth, but mostly for his children. Frank wouldn't stand by and see his children grow up without a father.

"I just got off the phone with Hunter." He told Elizabeth as he come out of the den. "He's coming over for dinner. We can discuss the new lead and he has some information for me, too. Hunter suggested I find another place to stay until this is all cleared up." Frank knew Elizabeth wouldn't want to hear the last part, but he knew she would handle it well. He a lot of faith in her.

"Where are you going to go?" Elizabeth asked.

"I'm not sure, but I don't want you to know. I don't want you to have to lie to the police."

"I understand. I will make sure things go smoothly as they can for everyone here. Don't worry we will be okay. I'll make sure I do everything I can for John and Phyllis."

"Lizzy, please keep the police away from them. They are finally starting to fall into a comfortable routine."

"I will do my best." Elizabeth took a deep breath, "This is so hard on all of you. I hope it will be over soon." She wanted to keep things as positive as she could for Frank. It wasn't easy. She was scared for him and afraid she wouldn't do a good job. But Elizabeth knew, deep down, she would do the best she could. Her best had always been go enough.

Packing Frank's bag, Elizabeth included a little of this and that, not knowing all he would need. "Can I pack you some food?"

"I'll take care of the food. I want you to go to our bank, but not our branch. The one across town. Please take out five hundred dollars in small bills." Frank said.

"Okay, is there anything else I can pick up?" Elizabeth knew Frank wanted to float below the radar and the police would be monitoring his accounts.

"No. Please take the money to this address. It's a mailbox store. Buy two envelopes and stamps. The police will be watching you. Let them see only one. Put these strips of paper in it. Hopefully, the police will think it's the money. Put the envelope into P.O. Box 152. Here's the key. If it works the police will stay and watch the mailbox. That will give you a chance to mail the real money to Officer O'Conner at this address."

"Okay. I love you." Elizabeth looked deep into Frank's eyes, and without speaking a word told him: It will be okay. I love you, more than words could ever convey. No matter how things turn out, I will always be here for you. With that she bundled up Sabrina, kissed Frank and left, hoping it would all be over soon.

This was hard for her. It was against everything she was ever taught. You respect the law and run to it in times of need. Not from it. Trust it. Elizabeth learned the hard way, the law doesn't always work the way it was intended. There were too many variables.

Back at home Frank got his gear together. He felt blessed. It was a very turbulent time in Frank's life, and he finally had someone that would stand by him, no matter what! He took one last look around. He didn't know the next time he would see his home or family.

* * * * * * * * * * * *

Later, after Elizabeth ran her errands, which worked like a charm, she picked up Phyllis and John. "How was school?"

"It was okay…" John seemed very down. It was rough on him. John wanted to get to know his father and have a normal life. He was losing interest in school, and his grades were beginning to show it. Phyllis on the other hand, had never had such high marks. She was working extra hard; trying to lose herself in her work. But with all the work at school and pushing to do extra chores at home, Phyllis was becoming exhausted. Elizabeth was getting very worried about the children.

CHAPTER 17

Frank proceeded to his meeting place with Officer O'Conner. Soon as he arrived, Frank and O'Conner started to discuss the case. Between the two of them all the facts seemed to be in. Some things about the case were still troubling Frank. The facts didn't point to anyone on either of their witness or suspect lists, but the answers were there somewhere.

It took hours to work through all the paperwork. Officer Hunter O'Conner discovered an interview Frank had done. It was one with Ms. Thatcher. The interview was very concerning to both of them. It was decided they would come up with a few more questions. Hunter would go out on a limb and start following up this new angle. Hoping it would be the new lead to crack the case.

"Are you sure you want to risk it?" Frank knew Hunter could get into trouble with the police force if they ever found he was helping Frank and concealing his whereabouts.

"Yes, I do. It's too dangerous for you out on the street. I know you are innocent! The sooner we can prove it; the sooner you can turn yourself in."

"I agree with that! I hate this hiding crap." Frank said, hoping they could find out who killed his ex-wife. He just wanted to get this all behind him.

Hunter went to the home of Sarah's best friend, Ms. Thatcher. There he asked her if she knew anything about Lt. Jorgenson's wife.

"I only know he was afraid of her."

"Lt. Jorgenson was afraid of his wife, or just afraid she would find out?" Hunter was surprised that Lt. Jorgenson would be afraid of a woman from all the things he had learned about him.

"He *was* afraid of his wife! I remember, Sarah made a comment the next time we talked, after she found out about his wife and broke it off. 'It was almost funny the way she scared him'." Ms. Thatcher commented.

Hunter thanked Ms. Thatcher   for the information and left. He found Lt. Jorgenson's address and went to have a chat with his wife.

Mrs. Jorgenson was hateful and very uncooperative. But in her state of anger and hatefulness, she made a slip. Mrs. Jorgenson always claimed she had never met the woman her husband was having an affair with, but this time she said, "Even in college she was a man stealer." Mrs. Jorgenson was speaking of Sarah!

Hunter pretended not to notice the discrepancy. Thanked her for her time and left. He immediately went to Frank. Frank gave Hunter the name of the college Sarah attended. After some checking, Hunter found Sarah and Mrs. Jorgenson attended college at the same time, sharing some of the same classes.

Officer O'Conner got a list of their classmates and found the ones that knew both Sarah and Mrs. Jorgenson. He interviewed many of them. The results of the interviews were very disturbing.

Most of the people remembered Mrs. Jorgenson as being a jealous person. Her jealousy wasn't just over the men in her life. It extended to wanting things others had. Including looks and portions of other people's personalities.

Not only was she jealous, she was a vindictive and conniving snake. Even her best friend worried what she would do to herself or someone else if she didn't get her way.

Mrs. Emily Jorgenson was not married when she met Sarah in college. She felt Sarah was prettier and more talented. Emily was majoring in accounting and felt it was not as important as Sarah's law major. In the years following college, Emily continued to be jealous of Sarah and resented her.

Officer Hunter O'Conner interviewed many people that knew Emily Jorgenson. She was found to be untrustworthy and a gossip. Many of the people she worked with were afraid she would stop at nothing to get their job (if it would move her up the corporate ladder.) They said Emily was a back stabbing, double-dealer.

Hunter decided he had better find out who Emily's friends were. In talking to many people who knew her, he found she had very few friends. She had her best female friend and a couple of male friends. Emily's best female friend was very candid about her.

"I know I don't seem to be much of a friend, but Emily isn't the nicest person to know. Why we are still friends after all these years, I'll never know. I guess she is just convenient, and I would *never* want to be on her bad side. When she likes you, or is pretending to, Emily is very extravagant."

"I am afraid to tell you how she is. I don't know what she would do if she found out I was bad mouthing her… But I can't stand by and allow people to think she is sweet! Emily was jealous of Sarah all throughout college and beyond."

"I know what happened the night of Sarah's murder, but I am very afraid!" Emily's friend was crying and visibly shaking. "Can we go to the station? I would love to tell someone my story. If we go right now, can you protect me?"

Officer O'Conner reassured her he would. He was very happy to take her to the police station so she could make a statement. Hunter called Frank to tell him the good news. He told him to go home and sit tight. On the way he radioed in so an interview room would be waiting.

Soon as Emily's friend and Officer O'Conner were at the station they were ushered into an interview room. With tapes rolling, Emily's best friend told the whole story.

"It started the first day they met, during freshman registration. I went with Emm... I mean, Emily. Soon as she saw Sarah, she started comparing herself to her. Emm saw Sarah as perfect and felt she was going to be a lot of competition. Emily quietly kept tabs on her. Every time Sarah had a success Emily would get angry. Her anger and jealousy slowly turned into an obsession. One that she carried past college."

"When Sarah married Frank, Emily became enraged. It meant that she won 'The Who Got Married First' portion of this made up competition. Then time went by and Sarah had a loving husband and two loving children. Emily felt Sarah's life was perfect. This consumed Emm to the point she wasn't dating… Didn't even have a social life." Emily's friend said with distance in her voice. After a thoughtful pause, she continued. "When Emily heard of Sarah and Frank's divorce. She was ecstatic. Emily started to find herself, and began to let go of her obsession."

"Soon after, she met and married Mr. Jorgenson. Now she was happy. She was in control, married to a man she felt worshipped her. And, most important, she was married, while Sarah divorced."

"Everything was going along fine until Emily found out her husband was having an affair. She was downright scary when she found out he was seeing Sarah. Even though she knew, her husband was completely unaware of the connection between Emily and Sarah. She was angry at Sarah even though Emily knew Sarah wasn't aware Mr. Jorgenson was married. So she started obsessing about Sarah again, and began dating another man by the name of Robby. Emily only dated Robby to get back at her husband. Things were going okay, but Sarah found out that Mr. Jorgenson was married and broke up with him. Instead of Emily being happy, in her twisted mental state, she took the break up as Sarah's way of saying she was too good for Emily's husband. It didn't make any difference that Sarah didn't know who Mr. Jorgenson was married to."

"Emily had such a strong hold on Robby. She convinced him they should get Sarah out of the way. Emily went by Sarah's house saying she was looking up college classmates. Then Emily and Robby watched her house to figure out her schedule. During the day of the night they killed her, they saw the children leaving with overnight bags. That night, when she was alone, they snuck in with a steak for the dog. Emily had befriended the dog during her many visits when Sarah and the children weren't home."

"Robby jimmied the back door open. They went in, killed her, and left the same way they entered. The next day Emily bragged to me about it. I wanted tell someone, but I was afraid she would kill me too."

* * * * * * * * * * * * *

After Emily's friend's statement Officer O'Conner called Frank and asked him to come and turn himself in. With Elizabeth at his side, Frank turned himself in. He spent a week in jail waiting for his hearing.

When he went before the judge his family was right there with him. Frank was found to be guilty of violating the terms of his bail and evading authorities, but was acquitted of all other charges. The judge sentenced him to time served and one year probation.

With Sarah dead and Frank acquitted of her murder. Custody of Phyllis and John was awarded to Frank. Elizabeth, with their blessing, legally adopted the children.

Now it was their time to live life as a family. Frank began many projects around the ranch he had put on hold during the investigation. Elizabeth took care of their home and family. Phyllis worked with her father learning about country life, and helped Elizabeth care for Sabrina and the new addition. John became the son he started out to be, before the divorce. He was his father's best assistant and closest friend. John came out of his shell, made friends at school, and started improve his grades. Everyone was beginning to heal. Soon they were all enjoying life, together.

Patricia Thompson (1973-) is a devoted mother of three independent teenage girls, and wife of a retired member of Search and Rescue. She grew up in Portland, Oregon. After high school she lived in Texas, California, Arizona and now resides outside of Portland with her family on their twenty acre ranch.
Mrs. Thompson spends most of her free time writing. Although this is her first publication, she is planning to publicize more in the future.